THE PARIS MANUSCRIPT

THE PARIS MANUSCRIPT

A NOVEL

Joseph Goodrich

Perfect Crime

Email: Crime@PerfectCrimeBooks.com
Perfect Crime Books™ is a registered Trademark.
Printed in the United States of America.

Parts of this novel first appeared in *Alfred Hitchcock's Mystery Magazine*. I'm indebted to Editor Linda Landrigan and Managing Editor Jackie Sherbow.

I'm happy to acknowledge the advice and assistance of the late Gordon McAlpine and of Nick Faust, Gordon Dahlquist, and Honor Molloy.

The epigraph from *The Captive* is taken from the Moncrieff/Kilmartin/Enright translation.

The quotation from Proust's 1907 letter to Georges de Lauris was translated by Richard Howard.

Cover art: Kevin Egeland

Library of Congress Cataloguing-in-Publication Data
Goodrich, Joseph
The Paris Manuscript

ISBN: 978-1-935797-944

First Edition: April 2022

For

Mick and Max Collins,

The gentlemen from the City of Light

We know that each murderer, individually, imagines that he has arranged everything so cleverly that he will not be caught, but in general, murderers are almost always caught. Liars, on the contrary, are rarely caught, and, among liars, more particularly the woman with whom we are in love.

Marcel Proust, *The Captive*

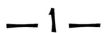

April 26, 1979
93 River Road
Point Pleasant, PA

I've been falling...

I'd tried to keep Annabelle from visiting. I put her off as long as I could, but she finally wore me down.

She arrived with a cake — my 85th birthday was fast approaching — and raised a fuss about the state of the refrigerator and the stove and the dust and the clutter and wondered how I could live in all this mess. I told her it was my mess and I was happy here and if she didn't like it, she could leave.

Annabelle didn't leave. She cleaned the kitchen and aired out the rooms and vacuumed the rugs and threw out all the old papers and junk mail and did the laundry and mowed the front lawn and the backyard.

And then, the day before she was scheduled to go back to Amherst, I was coming back from the bathroom when I felt dizzy. I'd almost reached the bed when I fell. Annabelle heard me and came bounding up the stairs into my bedroom.

She found me in my old pajama bottoms, sitting on the bedroom floor, staring at the toes of my slippers, tears falling onto the brightly colored rag rug.

She gasped when she saw the bruises on my arms and ribcage.

"Dad," she said, "what's happened? How did you get those?"

I've been falling…

She helped me up off the floor and onto the bed and gently wrapped an arm around my shoulder. I told her about the dizzy spells. I told her I'd stopped driving. Not because my license had expired and I was afraid I wouldn't pass the test – although I *was* afraid – but because I wasn't sure I'd be able to find my way home. I told her I'd arranged to have groceries delivered so I wouldn't have to risk the roads to Frenchtown. I told her I was getting along fine, and if I fell once in a while, I was still able to get up and get on with my life.

I felt old and foolish. The tears started again.

"Don't cry," she said, squeezing my hand. "It's okay."

It wasn't. I'd seen my future. I knew it was goodbye to the house, goodbye to all the years I'd lived here with Anabelle's mother, with my Daisy, after we'd come back to America from France and Annabelle was born and grew up and we grew old and Daisy died and I got older and older and started falling.

I wasn't crying about the future. I was crying about the past. It's been disappearing for some time. I couldn't see Daisy's face anymore.

No matter how hard I tried, I couldn't bring Daisy's image back to my mind.

Photographs were no help. They didn't look like her. I couldn't see the connection between the woman in the photograph and the woman I was trying to remember.

I was losing her again.

Eleven years ago, cancer wasted her to nothing, taking the light from her eyes and replacing it with the gaunt stare of the dying. It stripped away her beautiful hair and turned the naked scalp to parchment. One Tuesday night, cancer stole into her Doylestown hospital room and stilled her heart. Even as I'd held her, Daisy had slipped into death's arms and out of mine.

Imagine losing the one you love most in this world.

Then think of going through it twice.

"Dad," Annabelle said, as if the thought had just occurred to her, "how about coming to live with me and Jim? I think it'd be kind of nice. Don't you?"

4

I told her I'd consider it. She didn't push the issue. We finished our game of gin rummy, then I went off to bed and Annabelle sat by the fireplace and read for a while.

Staring at the ceiling, waiting for sleep to come down, I felt the weight of the years. It happens so suddenly, old age, or that's the way it feels. In truth the losses are so gradual one hardly notices them. When did the elasticity and strength of muscle disappear? When did names and faces start slipping away? When did the past triumph over the present?

You're exaggerating, I told myself. You're indulging in self-pity, and that was the one thing you've always tried to avoid doing. Straighten up and fly right, old man...

I had to smile. "Straighten Up and Fly Right" was playing on a jukebox in a joint on Lexington and 42nd when, over martinis, Daisy and I decided to move to Point Pleasant. We were tired of subways and noise and the eternal press and crush of seven million people; more importantly, we had a little girl to raise. We both agreed it'd be better for Annabelle to grow up near the city but not in it. We'd always wanted a house; the opportunity was presenting itself. What to do? Stand pat – or leap? We leapt.

And never regretted it.

"You've thought about it?" Anabella said.

"I have."

"And?"

"I'd prefer to stay here."

She started to speak, then stopped. Annabelle was always impulsive, a trait she shared with her mother, but she was trying her best to remain calm and logical.

"Okay," she said casually, and started for the kitchen. "So tell me: speaking of preferences, would you prefer potatoes or carrots with the steak tonight?"

Late Sunday morning. Breakfast and the paper had both been consumed. Annabelle was working on the crossword. She set her pen down – she's so smart she does them in ink. "That's what we could do."

"About what?"

"We could put some of those bars up. You know, in the bathroom. On the stairs. For you to hold onto."

"I don't need those things."

5

"You've been falling. It might be a good idea."

"They're a waste of money."

"You could hurt yourself if you're here alone. You *have* hurt yourself. I've seen those bruises."

"It doesn't happen all the time."

"It doesn't have to. Fall down the stairs and you'd kill yourself."

"I'm not falling down any stairs."

Annabella went inside and poured another cup of coffee, then brought it back to the little side porch where somnolent bees floated lazily through the greenery surrounding us.

"Think of it like this." She drank, then set her cup down. "You stay here all by yourself. One day – despite your best efforts – you *do* fall down the stairs. Or, God forbid, you have a stroke. Then what?"

"I die."

"Or wind up in some nursing home. If you're lucky."

"Would that be so bad?"

"You'd hate it."

"I hear some of those places are very nice."

"Jim's mother was in one for almost a decade, and I'm telling you: you wouldn't be happy."

I watched a hummingbird take delicate sips from the sugar water dispenser on the side of the house. "Beautiful, isn't it?"

"Is what beautiful?"

I pointed. "Your mother loved them."

"She had a real feel for nature, didn't she?"

"She had a knack for it. So do you."

We watched the hummingbird fly away, headed wherever hummingbirds go.

Anabelle placed the silverware on the plates and carried them inside. I heard water running in the sink and the clatter of metal on china. I lifted myself out of the chair and followed her in.

"I'm not trying to be difficult," I said to her back.

"You never *had* to try," she said, without turning around.

I shuffled past her into the living room.

"Which one is you?" Annabella said.

I moved the magnifying glass over the old photograph. "I'm not sure." I pointed at one of the soldiers lined up in front of a railroad station. "That's Jim Bower. He was from Oklahoma."

"Remember where?"

"...No." I tapped another soldier with an index finger. "That's Wisey the Wop."

Anabella gave me a look. "Who?"

"Wisey the Wop. He was Italian."

"I *know* that. But you can't say that these days. It's not considered polite."

"Everyone called him Wisey the Wop."

"That was sixty years ago. Times change."

I swept the photos into a pile. "Fine. You don't want to look at the pictures, I'll put them away."

She placed her hand on mine. "I'm not criticizing you. You know that. Right?"

"I guess."

She drew a photo out of the group. "So – which one is you?"

I studied the sepia-toned faces for a long moment.

"Dad?"

I set the magnifying glass down. "I don't know."

"You don't?"

"...No."

She gently touched one of the doughboys. "Right there. That's you. My brave and gallant father."

"I wasn't so brave."

"I've heard different."

"Brave, who can say?" I lifted a hand, let it fall. "Gallant, maybe..."

"I've heard that, too." She kissed me on the cheek. "From the very best sources."

Eventually, of course, she won me over. Or wore me down – I'm not sure which; like her mother, once she set her mind on a course of action, she followed it rigorously, not stopping until she'd realized her plan. Truth to tell, I'm deeply grateful for the love and concern she lavishes on the crotchety old man I've become. I'm lucky. I've not been tossed into some living-death house of a nursing home. I've not been thrown out onto the street. Taking everything into consideration, my health is good, my physical ailments few. I have no cause for complaint.

But when did that ever stop me from complaining?

Here I am.

I sit in this empty house in the shadows of a cool spring evening. A fire burns in the hearth. Tomorrow Annabelle and I leave for Amherst where I'll live with her and her husband Jim and be loved and cared for and hate every minute of it.

There I go again, exaggerating. I'm sure it'll be lovely.

It'll have to be.

All the necessary arrangements have been made. My papers have been arranged and boxed and are ready for shipping to my alma mater, a small college in the Midwest. They asked for the papers a while ago. I'm a historical figure by some standards, a living relic of a bygone era, one of a shrinking number of survivors from 1920s Paris. A lot of old friends and a few old enemies have received a great deal of attention of late. I see their names in the papers or in books at the library. I don't begrudge them the attention, but I don't read the books or the articles. I don't want to be famous just because I'd *known* someone famous.

I sit at my cleaned-out desk, the one we shipped back from Paris in 1940. I make these notes with the familiar fountain pen. When I pause to search for a word, I look out over the back lawn to the Delaware canal. I feel myself dissolving into the dusk. All is grey. I feel nothing. I *am* nothing — nothing but the fragile container of a few thoughts and habits that will soon disappear.

Like this life.

Like my Daisy.

And our life of love.

The fierce electric shock of it!

I am transformed. The fog has lifted. I feel the skin prickling on my arms and the back of my neck and the heart pumping in my chest.

I feel like Lazarus, brought back from the dead. Like someone who can *raise* the dead.

Last night I couldn't sleep, so I tossed aside the rumpled sheets and went for one last tour of the house. I started in the attic and wound up in my basement workshop. The hammers and chisels had been removed from their pegs, the paintbrushes and paint cans thrown away. The room was empty.

Except for an old trunk pushed far back under the workbench.

I dragged it out into the light. The trunk was furred with dust and cobwebs. I used a paint-stiff rag from a shelf above the workbench to give the trunk a dusting. The lock was broken and the trunk opened easily.

Inside were envelopes bulging with manuscripts, articles and book reviews I'd written, and a half-dozen boxes containing photographs, postcards and souvenirs: a pair of maracas from Mexico, a menu from the *S. S. Paris*, a doll from Capri.

I pored over the contents of each box and photograph album. The chill of the basement seeped into my bones, but I didn't go back upstairs.

Nothing could have torn me away from sorting through the scattered pieces of a life.

Yet none of it meant a thing.

The photographs were as dead as the people in them — just scraps of paper, conveying nothing. The souvenirs and postcards came from trips I couldn't recall. All was lost but the void.

At the bottom of the trunk lay a long, narrow leather box, the leather cracked with age. I opened it and found —

Daisy.

Marcel described this phenomenon of the past suddenly recaptured as involuntary memory. In *Remembrance of Things Past,* the narrator experiences it when he tastes a madeleine dissolved in tea.

For me it was the look — the feel — the faintest scent of lavender — of Daisy's white satin opera gloves.

I was no longer kneeling on the concrete floor in the basement of an empty house. I was no longer a lonely old man, mind fraying at the edges.

I was in Paris with my darling.

She removes the stopper from a bottle of perfume and places a drop in the hollow of her throat; then a drop on one wrist, which she rubs with the other. In a moment the scent of lavender rises in the room. Daisy reaches for her opera gloves, which are draped over the edge of her dressing table. I watch her pull one glove on, then the other, rolling and smoothing the satin along her forearms, holding her hands out to study them in the tremulous gaslight of our bedroom on the Rue Daguerre.

Pleased with what she sees, she turns to me and smiles. For that heart piercing instant, we are reunited. And then she was gone.

I wept. With sorrow, yes. But also with joy. Daisy had come back to me.

Under the box with Daisy's gloves, resting on top of the tissue paper that lined the trunk, was a manila envelope. I undid the clasp and found a notebook — and a photograph fell out: a confident young woman in an evening gown stands next to a gawky young man in a tuxedo. He's terribly thin, with sensitive eyes behind Harold Lloyd spectacles, and a military-style brush cut. That young man is me. And there, with her crop of honey hair, slim of form and pale of skin, is Daisy.

The photograph captured us in a moment of conversation at a

10

party, each turned to the other, caught up in the sheer pleasure of being together. She is my world. I am hers.

I realized with a jolt that the notebook was mine. Its pages were fragile and the ink had faded badly, but I could still make out what I'd written in late April of 1919:

Dearest Love:
Here's what happened and why. Read it when you can.
Your Ned,
who only and ever loves you...

I rose unsteadily and brought the pages to my desk. The sky over the canal was a light gray when I finished reading. Rain had fallen before sunrise. I lifted the study's window to cool air and the smell of grass clippings. A groundhog nosed its way across the backyard. Newly minted, the day awaited.

Time passed as I thought of our years in Paris, and of the people we'd known there. I thought, of course, of Marcel.

Most of all, I thought of the time my wife committed murder.

April 27, 1919
Paris, France

I'm with the corpses again.

Slogging through the mud, crazed with hunger and thirst, my feet are raw meat in my boots. I stagger toward the barbed wire of No-Man's-Land. Each step leads me deeper into a stew of sewage and severed limbs. The gore rises over my boots and I'm sinking. My mouth fills with shit and maggots. The sky is an open wound. My head goes under. I can't breathe.

Daisy held me as I screamed, held me till I came to in our bed, came back to this world. I lay there sweating and panting. I clung to Daisy, to her warmth, until my breathing slowed and I left the ungodly mess of war raging in my skull. I'd thought the dreams were gone for good, but they'd returned over the last couple of months. The punishing schedule at the newspaper and the roiling emotions of the short stories I was writing had taken their toll. The crypt of war had reopened, unleashing its terrors. I felt weak and broken by these dreams. And deeply ashamed. What kind of man was I? Why couldn't I control my mind?

"I don't know why you stay with me," I said. "You could have anyone you want."

"I don't want anyone else. I want you." She pulled me to her and kissed me. "Try to get a little rest."

"If *Collier's* would just buy another story, we'd be in silk."

"We could pay the rent."

"We could pay the butcher. And the baker."

She laughed. "I'm glad we don't owe anything to the candlestick maker, or we'd really be in the soup."

15

Talk of money had destroyed any chance of getting back to sleep. I kicked the sheets away and wearily swung my legs out of the bed.

"Don't get up." She reached out a hand. "Come back to me."

"Got to get to the paper."

"They can do without you for a few more hours."

"They can't."

"For God's sake, Ned, would you listen to me? You're falling apart."

I shuffled down the hall to the bathroom. I heard the concern in her voice – and the irritation. The nightmares had turned me into a pallid version of myself. I'd dropped a lot of weight. I was seized by tremors and shook uncontrollably. Voices babbled faintly in my ears. I was drinking too much at the bar around the corner from the paper's offices; drinking too much everywhere. I jumped at the sound of an automobile backfiring or the squealing brakes of the Metro. I'd nearly decked a stranger for bumping into me on the street. I'd yelled at Daisy – God help me for it.

"God help me," I said to the reflection in the bathroom mirror.

I didn't believe in God, but here I was, asking for his help – a sure sign of how low I'd sunk.

I rested my forehead on the cool glass of the mirror. Waves of exhaustion rolled through me. I ran hot water and put my shaving brush in the basin to soak for a few minutes, then started for the kitchen. I was sleepwalking with open eyes. Each step took an eternity. I might never reach the kitchen. I might be dead and not know it. That struck me as funny, and I laughed – the first time in weeks. I opened a kitchen cupboard and reached for cups and coffee.

"Ned…"

Draped in my tatty paisley robe, Daisy stood in the kitchen doorway. Hair tousled, sleepy-eyed, barefooted, she made that robe look like it came from Sulka's. A pang of desire stirred in me.

"Please don't get upset, but…" She sat at the table by the window. "You're killing yourself and you're killing me. I can't take it any longer."

I placed the coffee pot on the stove. "You'll have to. At least till the conference is over."

"That's months from now."

"I don't set the schedule."

"The paper's running you into the ground and you're letting them."

I whirled around. "Look, if I –"

16

I bit back my words. It took some effort. I couldn't stand to be questioned or contradicted. My anger flared like a grass fire. I tamped it down – only to have it burst into flame somewhere else.

I could ask Daddy to lend us –"

I slammed a fist on the stove. The coffee pot jumped. "*No.*"

"I'm not wild about the idea either, but he'd help us."

"I'd jump off the Eiffel Tower before I took a red cent from your old man. He hates me."

She sighed. We'd been through this before. "He doesn't hate you, Ned."

I choked back a gush of rage and stormed out of the kitchen. I furiously stirred a mug of shaving cream in the bathroom. I silently cursed Daisy's father, a Shanty Irish son-of-a-bitch who'd struck it rich late in life and thought he was John D. Rockefeller, tossing dimes at urchins.

The warm lather was comforting. I drew the razor methodically over cheeks and chin and throat. How easy it'd be to slice the jugular and let my problems bleed into the sink.

I hadn't reached that point yet.

I took a clean shirt and a fresh collar out of the dresser, put on my rumpled tweed suit, tied my tie with shaking hands, buttoned my vest. I studied the bleary figure in the mirror. The corpse was presentable.

Daisy was still in the kitchen. I poured two cups of coffee and placed one in front of her. She didn't acknowledge it. She avoided my eyes and stared into the street below. At the end of the block, a fat man in a blue smock and a beret waddled into Madame Sagan's *boulangerie*.

I sat across from her. We might have been two strangers at the opera. I got the coffee down as quickly as the heat would let me. It did some good.

"Drink your coffee before it gets cold," I said, lifting my hat off the peg. "I'm going now."

I waited for her to say something.

The fat man toddled out of the bakery, carrying a large white paper bag.

"Daisy."

The man took greedy bites as he wobbled along.

"I'm talking to you."

I swept the coffee pot into the sink with a clatter of metal, an explosion of coffee and a spray of grounds.

Only then did she look at me.

Her anger knifed me. She was as tired as I was – of our life here, of the eternal struggle to keep our heads above water, of the troubled and childish man she'd married. After six months of marriage this was all she had. This wasn't what she'd bargained for. Or what she'd been promised.

She got up without a word and left the kitchen. A moment later I heard the *snick* of our bedroom door.

I cleaned up the mess and left without saying goodbye.

At the paper I did what I always do: turn reporters' notes into serviceable prose. The Peace Conference was underway with new headlines every hour. A month after the Armistice, President Wilson arrived in Paris. The Allies – America, England and France – weren't as allied as they'd been during the War, when all they'd wanted to do was smash the Boche. France had lost millions of men and wanted to kick Germany's teeth so far down its throat it'd never attack anyone again. The Brits were terribly sorry that such widespread carnage had occurred but saw Germany as a possible market for English goods. America, led by the high-minded Woodrow Wilson, wanted to create heaven on earth – a fair and equitable peace that could not be broken.

Just when I thought I could trip the light fantastic out of the office, a report came in: street thugs had killed a representative from one of the Baltic States. The story kept me at my desk, waiting for reports to trickle in. It turned out be nothing but eyewash. I wanted to punch out my office windows. My waiting-around had been for nothing.

It was after seven when I capped my fountain pen, covered my typewriter, and dropped my green eyeshade into a drawer. I headed home to the Rue Daguerre for breakfast and sleep as the city eased itself into a new day. Waiters with tired eyes were hosing down the pavement and arranging chairs around tables outside of sleepy cafes. I nodded to an American who sat at one of the tables, a poet by the name of Hillyer. He nodded back and returned to his freshly-printed copy of the *Herald-Tribune*. The scent of baking bread drifted through the mote-filled sunlight. Closer to home I purchased a baguette and, just for a treat, a great sugary bag of chouquettes. I looked forward to curling up with Daisy and conking out. It didn't work out that way.

Daisy's brother Allan was seated in the kitchen, a glass of red wine in hand and a half-empty bottle in front of him.

18

"Little early for that, isn't it?"

"Or too late," Allan said.

"Are you back?" Daisy, wrapped in my paisley dressing gown, padded barefoot into the room. I gave her a kiss. She kissed me back. We did it again. Then she gently pushed me aside to start breakfast. "Go on," she said to her brother as she poured water into the percolator. "Tell Ned."

"I'm sunk." Allan polished off his glass and reached for the bottle, which I moved to my side of the table.

"Why don't you give your liver a rest and tell me what's bothering you?"

"I'm a dead man." Staring at the oilcloth on the table, teeth worrying his lower lip, he gathered his thoughts – and the strength to share them. The resemblance to his sister was striking; both were tall and lean with honey-colored hair. Allan had first arrived in Paris in 1917 as a cryptographer for the United States Military. He was now doing the same job at the American Embassy. He moved in diplomatic circles so we didn't see much of him. I liked him, though I didn't know him well. Daisy loved him unreservedly. He was her younger brother and she protected him with the ferocity of a mother lion.

"…There's this man," Allan said at length. "He – knows something about me."

"He does."

"Yes – but what he knows isn't as important as what he's done with that knowledge."

"And what's that?"

Allan looked up from the table, features tormented. "He's hounding me." He fought to maintain his composure but the pressure was too strong. He buried his face in his hands and sobbed.

Daisy stroked the back of his head and I poured him a glass of red wine. He needed it, no matter how early – or late – in the day it was. Wiping his face with a napkin provided by Daisy, he apologized for breaking down on us.

"Last year at an Embassy function," Allan said, "I met a fellow named Roy Carpenter. He's with the English legation. We both felt out of place there, and somehow we started talking. We became…friends."

"When was this?" I said.

"Last year. Around Christmas. We saw a great deal of each other after that. We were very discreet." He smiled ruefully. "For all the reasons I needn't explain. We were sure no one knew."

"But someone found out?" Daisy said, reaching into the icebox for the eggs.

"Yes." He produced an envelope from a jacket pocket. "Four months ago I received this."

I took the envelope. The return address, 3, Rue du Béarn, was written in rust-colored ink in a flowing hand – all very refined. The message was similarly tasteful, though its meaning was brutally clear.

My dear Mr. Herbert:

Romance is a lovely thing, is it not? And yet I fear
for those whose love is…unconventional. Should
the enclosed come to the attention of the larger
world – should it reach your employer, let us say –
the repercussions would undoubtedly be grave.

"What was enclosed?" I said.

"A photograph," Allan said. "Me and Roy in a little restaurant in Le Pré-Saint-Gervais. We were…embracing."

"Do you have the photograph?" Daisy asked.

"No. I burned it immediately."

"I wish you hadn't," I said. "It might have told us something."

"You can understand why I destroyed it."

"Of course we do," Daisy said.

"This calls you Mr. Herbert. Aren't you Mr. Lynch?"

Allan looked grim. "I changed it when our father kicked me out of the house."

I went back to the letter.

Surely such an unfortunate occurrence can be
avoided. I would be happy to keep your secret
friendship exactly that – a secret.

I hope this finds you and Mr. Carpenter well.

With my very best wishes,
*   Harry Burke*

I slipped the letter into the envelope and placed it on the table. "Charming little bastard, isn't he?"

"He's a monster," Daisy said.

"I assume another letter followed?"

"A week later," Allan said. "The worst week of my life. I couldn't eat. Couldn't sleep. Couldn't see Roy. I didn't want to take any unnecessary chances, so I sent him a *pneumatique* saying we should lay low for a while."

"What was in the second letter?"

"Burke wanted to meet me and suggested the Parc Monceau. We met at noon on a Saturday."

"When the Parc would be at its most crowded," Daisy said. "Very clever of him."

"What happened?"

"I got there early," Allan said. "But Burke was there earlier. He was sitting on a bench, throwing crumbs to the pigeons. He wasn't at all what I'd expected. Expensive suit. Medium height. Plump, with a great dark beard, very red lips, very white teeth. Quite jolly. We talked about everything but the photograph and the real reason we were there. I thought I'd lose my mind. Finally he got around to what he was after."

"Which was?"

"Financial considerations," Allan said with a sardonic inflection. "As a man of the world, certainly I knew the importance of remaining solvent in troubled times."

"How much of a financial consideration was he talking about?" Daisy said.

"A thousand dollars."

Daisy turned away from the stove, wooden spoon in hand. "You've got to be kidding. That's a fortune."

Alan reached for the wine bottle. I didn't stop him. A thousand bucks is a lot of greenery. If I'd been forced to cough that up, I'd be reaching for the bottle myself.

"You paid him?" I said.

"I had to."

"Where'd you get the money?"

"Half of it I'd saved." He emptied his glass in one gulp. "I sold some stock for the other half."

I poured coffee into a cup, added milk. "When did Burke come back for more?"

"A month later," Allan said. "How did you know?"

"Blackmailers always return."

Daisy whisked the eggs into a skillet. "How much this time?"

"Another thousand."

"What did you do?"

"Sold the rest of my stock and borrowed the rest. I didn't have quite enough, so I – I gave him my gold pocket watch."

"Grandpa's watch?" Daisy looked pained. "That's an heirloom. Please say you didn't give it to that man."

"I didn't have any choice."

"We'd have helped you if you'd told us."

"You and Ned have that kind of money?"

"No. But we'd have tried to find it."

"And the next time?" I said.

Allan poured the last of the wine into his glass. "A month later he asked for another thousand. I told him I didn't have it. I'd pawned or sold everything of any worth and there was no one left to borrow from. He suggested I pay him another way."

"What exactly did he have in mind?" Daisy said.

"He didn't...it wasn't *that*." Allan drained his glass and closed his eyes. "Burke suggested I borrow certain documents from the Embassy – papers relating to German war reparations – and let him see them."

"And that would be your payment," I said.

He nodded wearily. "That's right."

"Allan – no," Daisy said. Seeing the tortured look on her brother's face, she softened her tone. "I'm sorry. He had you over a barrel. I can see that. But I do wish you'd come to us."

"What kind of information did you give him?" I said.

"Nothing of any real importance."

"Still, you shared confidential papers with him."

"I know better now. I'll never do it again."

"That's not the point. He's got an even stronger hold on you now. And he'll have no qualms about using it."

"He already has."

"He's asked for more documents?" Daisy said.

"If he doesn't get them he's going to spill the beans about me."

"You believe him?" I said.

"I do. And that's why I'm going to kill him."

He spoke those words so matter-of-factly that Daisy and I were sure he meant it.

"As long as he's alive he won't leave me alone. He'll ruin me. He'll ruin Roy. I have to kill him."

Daisy moved toward him. "Listen to me. You can't —"

Allan rose unsteadily, knocking his chair over. He backed away from Daisy's outstretched hand. "He's turned me into a traitor. I'm going to kill him. Wipe him off the face of the earth."

Allan came to a ragged halt. His complexion was chalky. His lips moved but no words emerged. His eyes rolled back in his head. And then he collapsed.

Allan lay unconscious on the divan, a cold cloth on his forehead. Doctor Herrault, who lived downstairs, took Allan's pulse, listened to him breathe, and told us the young man was essentially sound and would recover nicely. He should get some rest and leave the wine bottle alone for a while. We thanked him and tried to pay. "But I have done nothing," he said and, suspenders dangling, returned to his breakfast. After he'd gone Daisy and I talked quietly as we watched Allan's chest rise and fall, rise and fall…

"Are you shocked?" Daisy said. "About Allan?"

"No. I knew."

Daisy looked surprised. "Since when?"

"A long time."

"I'd have told you, but Allan wants it kept secret."

"He doesn't have to — not here."

Daisy squeezed my hand. "Thank you. I was afraid you'd be shocked."

"The only thing that shocks me is that he'd contemplate murder."

"I've never seen him so upset. How do you think this Burke character found out in the first place?"

"How he found out doesn't matter. How to stop him does."

"Could you talk to Burke? Threaten him, maybe?"

"A threat only works if you can back it up. If I get tough, he could go to the police and blow the whole thing sky high." I stood up. "I'll think better when I've had some shut-eye. What are you up to today?"

"Painting sets for the Ballet Russes."

"I thought you were done."

"Pablo wants to make some changes. You know Pablo."

"Give that crazy Spaniard my regards."

Allan stirred, groaned, then sank back into sleep.

"Poor kid," I said. "He's in a hell of a fix."

"Do something, won't you, Ned? I'm afraid he really will kill that man."

"I won't let that happen." I gave her a kiss. "It's off to dreamland for yours truly. See you when you get back."

Waking up at five that afternoon, lying in bed with the sun pouring through the curtains, I let my thoughts wander. As I'd told Daisy, it wouldn't do any good to threaten Burke. But I had to do something, and the sooner the better.

By the time I was up and about, Allan was gone. He was a little worse for wear, Daisy said, but she'd calmed him down and bolstered his spirits. He wouldn't do anything rash, he said. I chose to believe him.

Daisy and I had steak and potatoes and a very decent bottle of red at the bistro around the corner. She shared the latest theatrical gossip and clued me in on what Picasso and Diaghilev were up to. It was all quite dramatic. She didn't press me for a solution to Allan's quandry, though she lamented the loss of their grandfather's pocket watch.

"He was a railroad man," she said. "They gave him that watch when he retired."

"Is it worth a lot?"

"It's worth a great deal, but that's not why I'm upset it's fallen into the hands of that despicable man. I'm upset because it belonged to Charles Arthur Lynch, who came to America as a teenager when his family died in the famine. Who worked his way out of poverty and raised a family that never knew hunger. That watch is proof of what he accomplished."

"No," I said. "*You* are."

"That's lovely of you. But I mean it, Ned. Fix that rotten blackmailer, or I'll kill him myself."

It was the end of another working night. I walked east along the freshly washed pavement until I reached the spacious Avenue d'Orleans. I turned right and headed north. I felt like something from a story by Jules Verne, a creature from under the sea.

The sun warmed me. The fresh air was good in the lungs. I began to feel better. I'd get some rest and wake in the late afternoon. Daisy and I would dine at the bistro on roast beef and asparagus, mashed potatoes and red wine. Then we'd go home and climb into bed. But not to sleep. I'd kiss the honey of her hair, her soft, giving lips, the hollow of her neck, her breasts, and we'd go to that place where the universe is gathered in one grand moment of harmony and peace.

Daisy was all I wanted, all I ever want.

Dreaming of love with eyes half open, half-asleep, I drifted through the waking city. The ancient buildings shone in the morning light. It was any and every morning in Paris. It was so beautiful I barely noticed the automobile.

It was a Citroen Type A Torpedo, idling at the corner of the Rue d'Alesia, near the Metro stop. I gave it a glance, admired its sleek lines, the promise of speed. If I had that car, I thought to myself, I'd be home with Daisy now.

Several blocks to the north, waiting for a junkman's cart to pass, I took a quick look around – and there was the Citroen.

You're being foolish, I told myself. *It's your imagination – that's all.*

I crossed the street, stepping quickly around the horse-drawn milk-wagons and vegetable carts, and entered the Rue Thibaud.

I darted a glance back. The Citroen kept pace with me. The first acid drops of fear entered my bloodstream. I was awake now. No more dreaming.

If the Citroen is still behind me when I'm halfway down the street – I'm being followed.

Picking up my pace, I examine my choices. I could head north – or double back to the south. Halfway down the block, I glanced back. The Citroen was there.

My heart ratcheted in my chest. Buildings loomed. The air vibrated with an ominous buzz. Voices whispered in my ears, warning me of danger. I wanted to run. My legs were rubbery. I might topple over at any second. I had to keep moving as if this were any other day.

Don't let them know you've seen them. Don't give yourself away.

The Citroen maintained a discreet distance, its pace geared to mine. I was fast approaching the western end of the Rue Thibaud. In a few more steps, I'd have to choose: North on the Avenue du Maine – or south.

North or south. Which?

I looked back again. A milk wagon was just turning into the eastern end of the street. In front of me, a slow-moving beer truck drawn by a quartet of massive Percherons was about to pass the western end.

A blockade, I thought. *Both ends of the street will be sealed and the Citroen trapped. A blockade – if you time it right.*

I bolted past the Citroen, swerved around the milk wagon and ran, nearly stumbling with each step, picking up speed and stability as I went. By the time the milk wagon and beer truck blockade had moved on and the Citroen was free to move, I was long gone.

The flow of adrenaline left me more depleted than ever. But I wasn't returning to our flat on the Rue Daguerre. If someone was following me, he might be watching me, too.

Across the street from our building was the café Daisy and I frequented. I slipped through the side entrance. Behind the zinc counter Jacques opened his mouth to speak. I held up a hand to silence him, nodding at the figure sitting at a table near the window. Old Jacques poured me a cognac. I placed a coin on the counter without making a sound, collected my cognac, and moved quietly toward the man.

A subtle shifting of position indicated that he'd heard me and was ready to fight or to fly, whatever the situation demanded. He was good that way. Always had been.

"Waiting for someone?"

The figure relaxed. It wasn't going to be a fight – this time.

"Goddamnit, Ned," he said, without turning around. "How'd you know I'd be here?"

I sat down across from him. "I didn't know it was you. But this is the only place on the street with a view of my building."

"Cautious as ever." He gave me his patented smile. I'd seen it a hundred times before. "How you been?"

"Fine, when I'm not dodging Citroens on my way home from work."

"Nice car, isn't it?" He stuck a thin green cigar in his mouth. "You're pretty fast on your feet. Always were."

"So were you."

He winked. "Still am."

I knocked back my cognac, signaled to old Jacques for another, and got down to the business of finding out why Lawson Peters was dogging my heels through the streets of Paris.

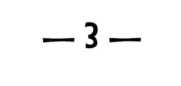
— 3 —

Lawson Peters. My old army buddy. I hadn't thought of him in years.

We'd fought together as doughboys during the Great War. I envied his ability to move through the world, trusting that his breezy temperament and Scandinavian good looks would pull him through any scrape. He envied my intelligence – or at least my schooling – and my ability to put words on paper. A scrapper from the streets of Chicago, he had little respect for the rules. I had too much. He knew how to get into trouble. I knew how to get out of it. We each had something the other lacked, and for a while there we were friends. We even wound up in the same army hospital in Deauville.

And we both fell in love with the same nurse.

The name on her passport was Julia Lynch. She was a tall, handsome Irish-American girl from the wilds of Brooklyn. She'd had a crop of whitish-blonde hair as a kid, so her folks nicknamed her Daisy. The years had darkened her mane to a honey color but the name stuck. Lean, lovely, with a devious sense of humor, Daisy wanted more out of life than circumstances allowed.

Her mother died shortly after Daisy's birth. When Daisy was still in rompers, her father remarried, started a second family, and parlayed a lucky bet on a horse into substantial real estate holdings along the Brooklyn waterfront. He moved the family from a cold-water flat in

29

Brownsville to the upper reaches of the Upper West Side. Money failed to mellow him; he remained a starchy, querulous figure given to rage and revenge.

After America's entry into the First World War, Daisy dropped out of college to join the Red Cross. Her father was furious – and even more furious when she chose to marry a guy with no assets, no connections and no future: me. He didn't care for me and I returned the sentiment.

I'd say I fell for Daisy the moment I saw her, and that might just be time talking. But shortly after meeting her I knew she was the kid for me.

Lawson got wounded first. A bullet in the shoulder had spun him around and knocked him into the muddy gruel of the trenches. By the time I reached the hospital, he was king of the ward. I can see him still, dressing gown over candy-striped pajamas, arm in a sling, playing dominoes in the rec room, laughing and cursing and scattering ash from the Celtique pasted to his lower lip. He and Daisy were an item, meaning they went for walks around the hospital grounds. Lawson was stuck on her pretty bad.

I arrived in far worse shape than Lawson. I was riddled with shrapnel and had pneumonia. Daisy told me later that the doctors had written me off. Even if I lived through the pneumonia, I might never walk again. Daisy got me through the pneumonia and up on my feet.

I'd beaten the odds, but I was miserably weak and bluer than a mid-summer Minnesota sky. I could see no light, no hope anywhere. Life wasn't worth the trouble it would take to end it. I lay in my hospital bed, barely eating, rarely talking. With humor and patience and doses of the salty language she'd picked up in the streets of Brownsville, Daisy brought me back to life. I realized I was in love.

And it was clear that Daisy loved me. Lawson cut me dead for the rest of his time in the hospital. He never said a word to me so I gave up on him. If that's how he wanted it, that's how he'd get it. I didn't need his friendship. He left the ward shortly after that and returned to the front. I received a letter from him a month later, apologizing for the way he'd behaved. I wrote back, telling him I was happy to hear from my old pal and hoped we'd have the chance sometime to shoot the breeze – but first, let's get the Kaiser.

Too frail to return to active duty, I was honorably discharged in early July 1918. By the end of the month I was back in Minnesota with no idea of what I'd do next. I lived in a cheap residence hotel in Saint

Paul and drifted from job to job, drinking too much, dreaming too much, achieving nothing. I wandered around in a tight-fitting French suit and Basque beret, criticizing the quality of American civilization. There were no real writers here and the food was terrible. The bread and coffee were better in France. *Everything* was better in France. *I* was better in France. Ernie Hemingway, an old sparring partner of mine, felt the same way about Italy. What our friends and family back home put up with! We must have been *insufferable*.

By this time Daisy was safe in Paris, working as a nurse in an army hospital. I lived for her letters and wrote her two or three times a day. Her letters made me laugh with her deft, dashed-off pencil sketches of people we knew. Salvation was found in every postcard and letter she sent. We poured out our hearts and started talking about what might happen after the war, for the Germans were licked by this point. The future beckoned. What should we do?

"I think the thing to do is come back to France and marry me."

This frightened *and* excited me.

My depressions, self-doubt, paralyzing fear of the opposite sex, the whole crippling mess of my childhood — all were proof positive of my inability to love and be loved. I had no skills to my name, just an obsession with moving words around on a page. Great fun, but no way to make a living. I was poison.

Daisy dismissed my reasons. "Is your love for me weaker than your fears for us?" she wrote. "There's nothing we can't meet together. Come to Paris, Ned. Come to me."

I was a moody wreck. But now I had something no one else in the history of the world had ever possessed: the love of my blue-eyed, honey-haired Daisy.

With her I would conquer all fears.

How to get back to the City of Light? Donald Ogden Stewart, a colleague in Saint Paul, got me a job as a foreign correspondent for one of the Minneapolis rags. In late October of 1918, I was on a steamship leaving New York harbor. The crowd waved from the pier, but I didn't see them. How could I?

I was looking at Paris.

— 4 —

April 27, 1919
Paris, France

The last time I'd seen Lawson Peters, he was in uniform, ready to return to battle.

Here he was soberly attired in a navy-blue, three-piece suit with high-cut lapels, bowtie, and a boater with a striped band. He looked prosperous, a man of substance. I wondered what line of work he was in.

Lawson reached into a coat pocket and withdrew a thin green cigar. "Cheroot?"

"Naw."

He struck a wooden match on his thumbnail and lit up. "You always were a clean-living lad." He exhaled a cloud of smoke. "Even during the War. So tell me – how's the peace treating you?"

"Fair."

"Still writing?"

"Now and again."

"I hear you move in some pretty rarefied circles these days." Lawson studied the tip of his cigar. "The Shelton-Drakes, for instance. Heard you and Daisy are good friends of theirs. That right?"

Our friendship with Sandy and Beatrice wasn't a secret, but it was strange hearing Lawson bring them up.

"We know them."

"I understand you're going to a party at their house tonight."

"How'd you come across that piece of information?"

"I work for the American Embassy. It's my business to know things." He ground out his cigar in the battered tin ashtray. "Let's stretch our legs."

I stayed seated. "My tail's dragging. Gotta get some rest."

Lawson adjusted his hat, shot his cuffs. "You'll want to hear what I have to say. It involves a young man who also works at the Embassy."

"Why should I be interested?"

"Because Daisy is."

"Is she really?"

"She's having an affair with him. I'd say that's a sign of interest."

We wandered through the Montparnasse Cemetery, surrounded by time-stained tombstones. If Lawson was right about Daisy, I belonged here, dead and buried in my grave.

Daisy wouldn't have an affair. The idea filled me with hurt and dread – and the fear that it might be true. God knows I was hell to live with. Trapped in a 24-hour nightmare, forcing myself through the day before I succumbed to sleep that offered no respite, I was a haunted man. I wanted to get up and walk away, leave the whole thing there. I didn't want to ask Lawson Peters a damned thing. But I did.

Who is he?

Lawson lit another of his thin green cigars. "His name's Allan Herbert."

I could have burst out laughing with relief. He evidently hadn't figured out that Allan was Daisy's brother. Something told me to keep silent, listen, and bide my time.

"He's been at the Embassy since January," Lawson said, "working as a code clerk, which keeps him pretty busy these days, what with the Peace Conference and all. Quiet type. Young fella, bit of a dude, works hard. Only one thing wrong with him, far as I can tell."

"Yeah?"

Lawson puffed out smoke. "He's a spy."

"...You're ribbing me."

"It's no joke," Lawson said. "I guarantee you."

"How do you know?"

"Allan Herbert's in charge of decoding certain documents about war reparations. How badly are we going to stick it to the Krauts? How much can we demand in damages? What can they pay? How will it affect the post-War economy? Some of these documents have turned up in the hands of the Germans. Nothing critical, thank Christ, but there's a leak, and it looks like this Herbert fella's the source. It's got to stop."

"Why don't you just arrest him?"

"There must be others involved. We want to catch 'em all."

"Where does Daisy come in?"

"We've had Herbert under surveillance. Daisy's been seen coming in and out of his apartment the last couple weeks. Makes a guy wonder."

"Where do I fit into this?"

"We fought together, Ned. I know your capacities. You're a straight arrow. I can depend on you."

"Cut the malarkey and get to the point."

"Herbert gets a new set of documents today. He's going to the Shelton-Drakes' party tonight. I want you there to keep an eye on him. See who he talks to, what he does. He's been seen in the company of a man named Harry Burke. This Burke's an Englishman who's lived in Paris for thirty years. There's something unsavory about him."

"Such as?"

"Hard to put a finger on it. He's been on the fringes of a lot of crooked deals but he's never been arrested for any of them. We're thinking he just might show up at the Shelton-Drakes'. They have an open-door policy when they throw a hooley. Burke could easily walk in, meet with Herbert, get the papers, and leave without anyone being the wiser." Lawson stopped to study a life-sized angel carved out of marble and placed on top of some luminary's grave. "I can't go to this shindig because Herbert would recognize me. He knows I'm in Security and might suspect something's up. But you're a friend of the hosts. You can go. Watch. Report back to me." He extracted a card from a silver case. "Here's my number. Call me soon as anything important happens."

"What if nothing happens?"

"We'll wait till the next time."

"What if I don't want to help you next time?"

"You're not helping *me*." Lawson brushed cigar ash off his vest. "You're helping Daisy. And, of course, the good old U.S.A." He clapped me on the shoulder. "Don't be a stranger." He ambled toward the cemetery gates.

"Hey," I called out.

37

He stopped and turned. "What?"

"Why follow me? Why didn't you just knock on the door and tell me what you wanted?"

"Common sense. I had to make sure you and Daisy weren't in this together. Wouldn't be the first husband-and-wife spy team." He lit one last thin green cigar. "Keep 'em flying, pal."

He strolled away, smoke drifting in his wake.

"There's a leak at the Embassy," I told Daisy. "They're pretty sure it's Allan."

Daisy looked stricken. "What can we do?"

"For a start – keep him away from Sandy and Beatrice's party. They think he's going there to pass along some new intelligence."

"To this Harry Burke fellow?"

"That's what they think."

"I'll tell Allan not to go. He'll listen to me. Though," she added ruefully, "it only postpones his problem."

"We can use all the time we can get."

"Burke will still want Allan to steal things. But you'll take care of it, won't you, Ned? You promised."

I gave her a kiss. "I'll take care of it."

I hoped it wasn't an empty promise.

The taxicab dropped us on the Quai de Bourbon. We passed through the entrance court. I lifted the brass lion's head and let it drop once, then twice.

The door opened to noise and light. Intricate strands of music rose in a vivid tapestry of sound. Mathilde took our coats and led us from the foyer into the Shelton-Drakes' large and ornately decorated living room.

A group of men and women, all in formal wear, were gathered around a lean and pale string quartet. We seated ourselves on a brocaded divan worth a year of my newspaper salary.

The tuxedo-clad musicians spun a shimmering pattern of notes. When the piece came to its conclusion, the audience applauded madly. A lithe dark-haired woman in a sleeveless evening gown gave us a smile: Beatrice. She'd already had a glass of two or champagne and was glowing.

"Heavenly music," she said. "Don't you love it?"

"We adore it," Daisy said. "Who's the composer?"

"Vivaldi."

"Kind of old-hat, isn't he?" I said.

"So old it's new again," Beatrice said. "Vivaldi's undergoing a revival, thanks to Ezra."

"Among others," said Alexander Shelton-Drake, appearing at his wife's side.

Sandy reminded me of a stage magician, with his waxed mustaches and saturnine manner. Beatrice was the girl in sequins and tights who gets sawed in half and then, hey presto, restored.

I've speculated a great deal on what drew Sandy and Beatrice together. He was a good twenty years older, but the difference in age didn't affect them. He had enough of the green stuff to fill an ocean liner – or to buy one – but Beatrice came from very plush circumstances herself and hadn't needed to marry for money. I attributed their mutual attraction to this: they were both fascinated – obsessed – with the *new*. Anything new, anything contemporary, from Einstein to the music of *Les Six*, was just their cup of tea.

Since leaving the world of business for the world of art, Sandy had written several novels, all very modern, very new. His books reminded me of the Scottish Highlands: difficult to get through, but impressive. "They must be good," he once said to me, half-joking. "They don't sell." Luckily he didn't have to depend on his earnings as a writer for his living. But he knew that other writers did, and he doled out large sums to a variety of artists – even Ezra Pound, with whom he'd had a monumental falling-out. But then, as Sandy liked to say, who hasn't?

"Will he be here tonight?" I asked.

"Highly unlikely," Sandy said. "Vivaldi's been dead for several hundred years."

"He means Ezra, silly," Beatrice said.

"Ezra *is* silly," Sandy said. "Half the time I don't know what he's going on about. He doesn't know a damned thing about money, I can tell you that."

"Except how to spend it," I said.

"There's no trick in that," Daisy said.

"There is if you don't have it," I said.

"Well, I do, and I like artists to have some, too," Sandy said. "Even Ezra, annoying as he can be."

"In for a penny..." Daisy said.

39

Sandy burst into booming laughter. "That's good, my dear, that's very good!"

"We *do* have a special guest this evening," Beatrice said.

"Who?" I asked.

"You'll just have to wait and see." She linked her arm in Daisy's. "I've been dying to talk with you. Pierre Auguste may show up tonight. You *have* to meet him. He's the editor of a new fashion magazine. Very stylish – the magazine, not Pierre. Though he does cut quite a figure. He'll *love* your illustrations."

Beatrice led Daisy toward the bar, where servants in white jackets filled and re-filled glasses. When they'd each received a glass of champagne, they took seats by the French windows. Sounds from the river, boats and people, drifted into the room.

"Quite the duo," Sandy said admiringly.

"Quite the duo," I echoed.

They were indeed. Daisy and Beatrice had grown up together. Nathanael Miller, Beatrice's father, was a well-to-do doctor in Brooklyn Heights who lived and worked in a brownstone on Willow Street. One day Beatrice brought him a dirty-faced little urchin with a broken arm: Daisy. She'd sneaked into the Millers' backyard to steal apples off their tree. She'd gorged herself and then – she'd slipped. Beatrice saw Daisy falling past her bedroom window and hurried out to save her. Dr. Miller set her arm, fed her lunch, and never asked for payment. It was clear from her torn frock and smudged face that Daisy's family were paupers.

The Millers liked Daisy. They relished her unruly spirit, her jokes, her intelligence. Beatrice kept Daisy's wild streak in check; Daisy helped Beatrice escape the straitjacket of conventional behavior. They were like sisters. "Better than sisters," Daisy once said. "We don't *have* to like each other. We just do."

Beatrice and Daisy went to Bryn Mawr. But shortly before they would have graduated, America entered the War. The Red Cross brought them to Europe – and to their future husbands. I met Daisy in a hospital in Normandy. Beatrice and Sandy met at an experimental music concert at the Salle Pleyel. The audience catcalled and booed and showered the stage with torn-up programs. Beatrice and Sandy had been the only ones applauding. From that instant on they were besotted.

Sandy went off to greet some newcomers. I spoke with a young painter who had his sights set on a commission from the Shelton-Drakes. I discussed baroque music with the lank-haired cellist from the string quartet. A woman from Antwerp told me about the horrible state of war-torn Belgium. After a time I found myself at the edge of a group with Daisy and Beatrice at its center.

"We never did anything very wicked," Beatrice was saying to her admirers.

"We read Balzac," Daisy said.

Beatrice waved that away. "That's not *very* wicked."

"That wasn't the point. The point was, we were absent without leave. If all we'd done was drink lemonade and play a few hands of bridge, it would have been worth it. Hello, pookie," Daisy said brightly. "Are you having fun?"

"Tons," I said.

"We were talking about our school days."

"So I gather."

"We weren't *very* wicked," Beatrice said.

"Maybe not," Daisy said, "but do you remember the time Captain Phelps had to escort us back? That wasn't an easy night."

A red-faced man with a crooked bow tie said: "What happened?"

"I don't think I can tell you the whole story," Daisy said.

"Is it rude?"

"Her husband's here," someone said, pointing at me.

"Ned's heard this story," Beatrice said blithely. "He doesn't mind."

"Is this the one where you wound up in Lake Waban?" I said.

"That's the one," Daisy said.

"Do you know all your wife's stories?" the red-faced man said.

"Every one of 'em."

"He puts up with all of my whims," Daisy said. "He's a perfect saint. Now – where was I? All I can say about that night is that it involved the State Police, a kidnapping charge, and a box of Lapsang Souchong tea."

"But it wasn't wicked," Beatrice insisted.

"Then what was it?" someone called out.

"A tempest in a teapot," Daisy said.

There was laughter from the crowd. Daisy smiled, pleased that her joke had landed. Someone bumped into me and spilled my glass of wine on the rug. An attentive waiter leaped into action, dabbing at the rug with a wet cloth.

"I am so sorry," said a white-haired man with a heavy-but-refined Teutonic accent. "Let me get you another glass."

"That's not necessary."

41

"Oh, but it is." Leaning in close, he added with great urgency: "With you I must speak. Please?"

What could I say? "Sure thing."

"Sure – thing?" he repeated, working it out. Then, suddenly understanding, his relief was enormous. "Ah, yes. Please give me your glass. Was it red or white?"

"Red. I'll come with you."

"Allow me to introduce myself. I am Albrecht Schneider."

"Ned Jameson."

"Yes, I know that," he said. "It is a very great honor."

We pushed through the crowd's lively conversations on the way to the bar.

"He's a big joke," a guest scoffed. A monocle glinted above his salt-and-pepper Van Dyke. "That's not music. It's nothing but noise."

"No, no, no," said the string quartet's cellist. "Stravinsky is a genius."

"He's an upstart crow." The man's fingers formed a beak opening and closing. "*Scraaak, scraaaaak, scraaaaaack!*"

A few steps more brought me to a ramshackle middle-aged man with a crushed felt hat and large rimless spectacles. "The dollar's never been stronger," he said to the drink-befuddled man beside him. His accent was pure Williamsburg – a Brooklyn boy, born and raised. "They'll be flooding over, mark my words. Hell, they're *already* flooding over."

"Who's flooding?" said the little man.

"Americans," cried the man in the crushed felt hat. "They're coming over by the boatload and they'll ruin it for those of us who came here to get away from people like them. You may ask, 'What proof do you have, Henry?' That's what you're thinking, right?"

"I'm not thinking anything."

"That's your Goddamned problem, not mine."

The bar was three-deep with thirsty guests. Schneider grimaced. "No good, these crowds."

"It's on the busy side."

"The balcony is nice. Fresh air would be not bad." Schneider reached an arm between two guests and accepted a glass from the bartender. "For you." He grabbed a glass for himself. We stepped through the French doors onto the Shelton-Drakes' balcony.

Schneider closed the doors behind us and we stood in the darkness. Muffled party sounds could be heard behind the glass.

Schneider broke the silence. "Mr. Shelton-Drake says to me that you are a newspaper reporter."

"That's right."

"It is a large newspaper?"

"Large enough."

"Many people it reaches?"

"It does."

"Ah, yes. Yes, yes, yes. Herr Jameson…" He clasped and unclasped his hands. "I own a company that makes silverware. These are hard times for the small man of business. This is why, when Sandy tells me you will be attending his party tonight, an idea comes to me – this is the man I should ask for help. Business is very bad, Herr Jameson. In addition, I have had some financial difficulties. I have responsibilities, I have debts – I wonder, frankly, if I will remain floating." Schneider paused to get himself under control. "What I am wondering, my friend, is this: Is it possible for you to help me get advertisements in your very fine newspaper for not a lot of money?"

"You mean advertising space?"

"Advertising space. Yes! I search for advertising space for my company, Schneider and Hacker Silverware, Incorporated. I am in charge of the business outside of Vienna. Is this something you could arrange? Any favorable terms you might be willing to dispense me with –" He stopped. "Dispense to me?" He shrugged. "My English – not so good."

"I catch your drift."

His expression clouded. "Drift?"

I scribbled the paper's telephone number on the back of an old receipt. "Ask for Yvette. She'll work something out."

Schneider took the piece of paper the way a communicant accepts the holy wafer. "This is *ausgezeichnet*. I will call this woman. Right away in the morning." He held out a card. "Many thanks for this. I stand astounded. In case you should wish to be of communication, please – take this."

I thanked him, pocketed his card, picked up my glass, and left the hapless Schneider on the terrace.

I refilled my drink, refilled it again after a while. Time passed in the way it always passes at these affairs. I wouldn't say I was getting drunk, but I was decidedly happy.

The room's atmosphere suddenly shifted and its pulse quickened. Who could excite such a response? A star of the flickers, maybe? Or one of the bigwigs from the Peace Conference. Whoever it was, the room was bubbling like Sandy's expensive champagne. Guests were gathered near the entrance to the living room.

Beatrice spotted me in the crowd and waved a bejeweled hand. "Ned!"

I sidestepped a thickset woman in a tiara and dodged an old gent in a tuxedo that might have been worn to celebrate the end of the Franco-Prussian War. Daisy, effervescent with champagne and the pulsing party, clutched my sleeve. We slipped past a trio of desiccated grandees, the crowd parted, and there was the evening's special guest.

Standing between Sandy and Beatrice was a man of shorter-than-average height with dark eyes that were simultaneously limpid and piercing. His skin was of a lunar whiteness, much whiter than his dingy kid gloves. Beneath his fine, prominent nose was a deep black mustache. His top hat was in need of a good brushing. He wore a black fur-lined overcoat over a disheveled tuxedo. He reminded me of Max Linder with a touch of Chaplin. He possessed Linder's grace and Chaplin's sorrowful air, but the overall effect was far from clownish. His features were refined and sensitive; here was a man of sadness and charm.

Marcel Proust.

He saw us approaching, and his look of habitual melancholy dissolved. "Ned! Daisy!" He wrapped his arms around us. "I don't believe it!"

"You *know* each other?" Sandy was clearly astounded by the warmth of Marcel's greeting.

"Of course we do," Marcel said. "What was that song we used to sing?"

"There were several," I said.

Marcel beat time in the air with one soiled glove and sang in what he thought was an American accent:

> *We've got a parrot in our house —*
> *Pretty Pol, pretty Pol, pretty Pol!*
> *We've got a parrot in our house —*
> *Polly wants a cracker now!*
> *Hear her swear like a trooper bold.*
> *`Remember, she is only two years old!*
> *We've got a parrot in our house---*
> *Pretty Pol, pretty Pol, pretty Pol!*

Marcel, Daisy and I exploded in a fit of wild laughter.

He wiped his eyes with a silk handkerchief. "It does me such good to see you, my darlings. I think of you often. Those terrible days in the hospital."

"What hospital?" Sandy said.

"I spent some of the War in Deauville," Marcel said. "The hotels were turned into hospitals for soldiers. I used to bring them cigarettes and books."

"And champagne," I said.

"And scrambled eggs," Daisy added.

"I'd forgotten about the eggs," Marcel said.

"You were a soldier there?" Sandy said to me.

"Ned's a hero," Marcel said. "He was badly wounded and decorated for bravery. We had many fine conversations. He is a rare creature. And his lovely wife is even more precious."

"How did you know we were married?" Daisy said.

Marcel shrugged. "You're wearing a wedding ring – I detect its presence under your glove – and you and Ned are here together. A simple observation." His dark-ringed eyes shone with merriment. "Your mutual attraction was never what one might call a deeply held secret."

"I was Ned's nurse," Daisy explained.

"She was good for what ailed me."

Beatrice laughed. "Evidently."

"If not for the ministrations of this angel of mercy," Marcel said, "dear Ned might not be here tonight."

"Your book!" Daisy said, struck by the thought. "How is it?"

"Oh, the book..." Marcel's expression was pained.

"An absolute masterpiece," Beatrice said.

"My readership is small," Marcel sighed, "but discriminating."

A stocky dowager who'd edged her way into the conversation threw in her two cents' worth. "Is this book of yours a novel, Monsieur Proust?"

Marcel weighed his response. "In a manner of speaking, yes. It is a novel that will, when all is said and done, consist of a number of volumes. The first came out before the War. The next is to be published in June – if I am lucky enough to live that long."

"What is it about?" the dowager said.

Marcel peered at the woman from under drawn brows. "In a word, Madame? *Perversion*."

Aghast, the dowager backed away into the crowd.

"You just lost a reader."

Marcel grinned at me. "On the contrary. I'd say her interest has been piqued. Beatrice, my darling, may I once again impose upon your kindness?"

"By all means, Marcel. How can we help?"

"A word with your cook is all I desire."

"Of course," Beatrice said, surprised. "That's easily arranged."

Proust shifted his attention to Daisy and me. "You will forgive me, my children? I desperately require this information for my book. It is the only thing that could draw me away from you."

"Strike while the iron's hot," Daisy said.

"You are too kind to one who treats you so shamefully. Until soon, my little ones. You must join me for a late dinner at the Ritz some evening." He shifted his attention to Beatrice. "If you please?"

Sandy led us to a couch. "I can't believe you know Marcel."

"He was very good to me in Deauville."

"To both of us," Daisy said. "Here's to Marcel." We lifted our glasses. "You know," she went on, "I don't think I've ever met anyone as intelligent as Marcel is. – Sorry, darling."

"I don't mind," I said. "It's the truth."

"He's frighteningly brilliant," Sandy agreed.

"I'm in love with his book." Daisy crossed one silken leg over another. "I've never encountered anything like it. Have you read it?"

Sandy leaned forward confidentially. "Don't tell Beatrice, and for God's sake, don't tell Marcel – but no, I haven't. I've tried half-a-dozen times with no luck. I get bogged down in the first twenty pages. I'm not a stupid man, but I'm ready to admit I'm missing something. What is it I'm missing? Can you tell me?" Having made his confession, he lit a cigarette and puffed out clouds of brooding smoke.

Daisy sipped her champagne and gathered her thoughts. "Marcel told that lady his book is a novel, but in my opinion, it's not. Marcel's book isn't so much a novel, although there is a story, as it is the…delineation – is that the word I want? The delineation of a sensibility, a consciousness."

"Sounds like tough sledding."

"Not when you've acclimated yourself. I had to start it three times before I got through it, but I came to find it…" She took another sip of champagne. "Mesmerizing."

"What's the story?"

"Nothing so very unusual. It's what Marcel does with it that makes it unique. It starts off with a boy in a French village. He's fascinated by certain people, certain places; even certain names have magical connotations for him. We learn about what he reads, about his family and his overwhelming love of and need for his mother. There's a marvelous chapter where he craves a goodnight kiss from her but is afraid he won't get it because a family friend named Swann is visiting."

Sandy blew a smoke ring. "Riveting."

"But it is!" Daisy set her champagne glass on the table. "You're immersed in the child's thoughts and come to identify completely with him. Will he get a goodnight kiss from his mother? The suspense is awful. You'd think you were reading *Fantômas*."

"Now you're talking. *That's* a book I couldn't put down."

"There's a long section that takes place before the boy was born and involves their friend Swann, who falls in love with a woman named Odette. She's a courtesan who puts him through the wringer. Swann's story captures the frenzy, the all-consuming nature of a grand passion. The poor man is driven to distraction by this temptress who haunts his every thought and upends his life."

"Is it racy?"

"It's more about the disappointment of love rather than love's fulfillment. Swann discovers when the fever of love has cooled that Odette isn't even the type of woman he's attracted to. Marcel is saying that love is an illness that feeds on itself and then expires. The loved one has very little to do with it. In the final section, the narrator tells us of his childhood love for Swann's daughter Gilberte. This also ends in disappointment."

"No story, and it ends sadly," Sandy mused. "How provocative – and modern. I'll have to give it another try. If it's as good as –"

Beatrice walked rapidly toward us, looking worried.

"Something wrong?" Sandy said.

"Is Marcel all right?" Daisy said.

"He's fine. That's not the problem."

"Then what is?" Sandy said.

Beatrice took his arm. "Come with me. You, too," she said to us.

"Where's Marcel?" I asked.

"In the kitchen," she said curtly. "At least that's where I left him."

Dodging and weaving, fighting to keep up, Daisy and I followed the Shelton-Drakes through the mass of partygoers.

Beatrice led us into a quiet side room. An unhappy-looking servant stood beside a divan. A well-dressed young man – not much older than twenty – sat indolently smoking a cigarette in an overstuffed chair. His homburg, overcoat, and gloves were neatly draped over a nearby end table. An older woman in a chartreuse evening gown and opera gloves turned to us. Her tone was imperious.

"It's about time, Sandy!"

"What in heaven's name is wrong, Winnie?"

"She pointed indignantly at the young man. "He took it."

Sandy looked puzzled. "Took what?"

"The dear old thing is sadly mistaken," the young man said lazily, then puffed out a stream of smoke.

"Don't think you can lie your way out of this," Winnie said. She indicated the servant with a plump hand. "*He* saw you take it. – What's your name?"

"Etienne, Madame," the servant said, polite but miserable.

The young man was unfazed. "Whatever you call him, he's lying. Ten to one *he* took it."

Etienne turned stiffly to Sandy. "Monsieur Shelton-Drake, please don't think –"

"Think anything you like," the young man said.

Winnie rode over the young man. "Don't listen to this wretched boy, this – "

Sandy raised a peremptory hand and growled: "Quiet, please." When the three had settled down, he spoke again. "First things first. Ned, Daisy, allow me to present Mrs. Winifred Lee. A dear friend of ours."

"How do you do," we said.

Her response was a preoccupied "How do you do."

"Now, my lad," Sandy said, "just who are you, and what do you have to say for yourself?"

"I am Prince Antoine de Toth," the sullen young man said as if everyone in the world knew that but us. "I am at present attached to the Hungarian embassy."

"He's a friend of Amelie Rochaud's," Beatrice said. "That's why he was –"

The door opened and Marcel peered in. "I beg your pardon. Am I interrupting?"

Beatrice waved him in. "Please join us. I think you may be of some help here."

Marcel's curiosity was piqued. "What is the problem?"

"That's what I'm in the process of finding out," Sandy said.

"This reprehensible boy was seen coming out of your cloak room," Winnie said in an aggrieved tone. "You saw him, didn't you, Amiens?"

"Etienne, Madame," the servant gently corrected her. "I noticed him, yes."

"And then," the woman continued, "not five minutes after that, I went to the cloak room to get an address for someone – I carry a little notebook with addresses and such – and I discovered that someone had taken a substantial sum of money I had in the pocket of my wrap."

"It wasn't me," the young man said.

Sandy ran a speculative hand over his beard. "You saw him leave the cloak room, Etienne? You're sure?"

"Absolutely, Monsieur. I was bringing a glass of seltzer to one of your guests and had cause to pass nearby."

"Then what?"

"At some point shortly thereafter, I was approached by Mrs. Lee, who was... distraught."

"I wasn't distraught," Winnie said. "I was *livid*. One doesn't expect to be robbed in the home of friends."

"Of course not," Beatrice soothed. "It's a horrible thing."

Hands clasped behind his back, Sandy approached the young man. "What do you have to say in your defense?"

"Not a damned thing."

"Watch your tone," Sandy said. "There are ladies present."

De Toth rose to his feet. "A thousand pardons." He bowed deeply, then sat down again.

"Had you been in the cloakroom?"

"I had, actually."

"For what reason?"

The young man hesitated. "I needed another handkerchief. I'd lent the one I had on me to a lovely young thing who'd spilled wine on her dress. I had a spare handkerchief in my overcoat. It sounds silly, I know. But that's why I went in there."

Marcel stepped forward. "Did you leave the stained handkerchief in your overcoat, Monsieur?"

"I didn't."

"Then you have both handkerchiefs on your person, yes?"

"That's right."

"May I see them?"

De Toth considered Marcel's question, then withdrew a white handkerchief blotched with red. "Here."

Marcel examined it. "And the other?"

The young man produced a second handkerchief – the duplicate of the first, but pristine, with no wine stains. Marcel looked at it, then returned it.

"I hope this settles the matter," de Toth said. "I'm sorry, Madame, if something was stolen from you. I must also apologize for my tone. I was unbearably rude. But as you see, I only went to the cloak room for a fresh handkerchief – not your money. Someone in my position has no need to steal pocket change."

I could tell that Winnie wanted to be assuaged, wanted the situation resolved. "I see that, yes," she said reluctantly, "but the money – if you didn't take it, then who…"

"I assure you it wasn't me. And I'll be happy to prove it."

He removed his jacket, held it by the coat tails, and shook it till its contents – a pack of cigarettes, a gold lighter, the two handkerchiefs, a slim leather wallet, and several calling cards – fell to the floor. He tossed the jacket onto the seat of a chair, then turned out his shirt pockets and his pants pockets; they too contained nothing. "Not a franc, not a sou, not a cent, Madame. Surely you can see that. Surely you trust your own eyes?"

"Perhaps," Mrs. Lee began, "perhaps I was wrong, but…"

"An honest mistake, Madame." He put his jacket on. "I did nothing to help the situation with my arrogant behavior." He picked his belongings from the carpet and tucked them back into his pockets. "Now, Monsieur Shelton-Drake, if you've no objection…"

Sandy roused himself from a doubtful reverie. "No. No objections whatsoever."

"Then I bid you goodnight." The young man started for the door.

"Prince de Toth?"

The young man stopped at the sound of Marcel's voice.

"Before you leave us, would you be so kind as to take off your shoes?"

"…Why?"

"I should like to inspect them."

De Toth looked at us. "Who is this man?"

50

"Monsieur Marcel Proust. Your humble servant."

The young man thought for a moment. "I've heard of you. You're that – that *novelist*." In de Toth's mouth the word was poison.

"You do me a great honor," Marcel said.

"I also hear you're an invert."

Mrs. Lee gasped. Daisy and Beatrice exchanged nervous looks. We all knew about Marcel's inclinations but we refrained from discussing them. If you loved Marcel, as we did, you accepted him as he was.

Marcel was unruffled. "What I am or what I am not has nothing to do with the matter at hand. More to the point is the fact that you are a crook. Your shoes, sir. Please remove them."

"This is ludicrous."

"Then you leave me with no other choice." Marcel took off his top hat and placed it, brim up, on the sofa. "Sandy, Ned – will you assist me?"

Sandy looked incredulous. "You want us to remove this fellow's shoes?"

"That is precisely what I want."

"Because?" I said.

"Because he has hidden the stolen money in one of them."

"You belong in an asylum," de Toth said.

"You may be right," Marcel said. "But that, too, has nothing to do with the matter at hand. I have no wish to use force if it can be avoided. I have no desire to rob you of what little dignity you possess. Therefore I shall ask you one more time. Will you please return the money you stole from the lady?"

The young man's eyes narrowed unpleasantly. "I didn't steal anything."

Marcel sighed. "Gentlemen?"

Sandy and I moved toward de Toth and dragged him, cursing and struggling, to the center of the room. Sandy wrapped him in a bear hug while I grabbed one of the young man's legs and wrestled his shoes off. I brought them to Marcel.

"Well?" Sandy said, breathing heavily from his exertions.

"Both empty," Marcel said.

"I *told* you," a red-faced de Toth gasped. "I didn't take the old bitch's money."

"What should I do with this lout?" Sandy said. "Let him go – or beat the hell out of him?"

51

"Neither," Marcel said. "Please remove his socks."

De Toth stamped hard on Sandy's foot and bolted for the door. I caught him by the collar and hauled him back. He stumbled into me and we both fell. I wound up straddling his chest and pinning his wrists to the ground while Sandy grasped a flailing foot and tore off a sock.

"Anything?" I said.

"No." Sandy reached for the other foot. "Stop kicking, damn you...There!"

"You got it?" I asked Sandy, who remained silent.

"Let him up, Ned," Marcel said.

I released de Toth's wrists and he crawled off and sat curled in a ball against the divan.

"I *told* you I didn't have it," he said, eyes bright with hatred. He rose shakily to his feet, stuffed his shirt into his trousers, then smoothed out his lapels and jacket front.

"My heartfelt apologies," Sandy began. "I'd no intention of –"

The young man waved away Sandy's words, then put his socks and shoes on. "Forget it. All I wish to do is leave you poltroons to your rancid celebrations." He favored Mrs. Lee with a wintry smile. "I hope you're happy, Madame. Your wrong-headed accusations have brought shame upon you and your friends. I should sue every one of you for slander and assault. Instead, I'll wish you all a tender and heartfelt goodnight." He rose and crossed toward the end table where his hat, coat, and gloves rested.

"Allow me," Marcel said, stepping between de Toth and the end table. He picked up the overcoat and held it out. De Toth, surprised but convinced that others would naturally choose to serve him, inserted one arm and then the other into his overcoat. He muttered a cold but polite "Thank you."

Marcel presented the young man with his homburg. Then he offered a glove to the young man, who took it and waited for Marcel to hand him the second glove.

And waited. And waited. And waited.

Brows drawn together, de Toth stared at Marcel. Marcel, smiling dreamily, stared back. The silence stretched on. And still Marcel did not return the glove. We waited, rapt.

The tension in the room increased with each passing second. And still Marcel, smiling dreamily, did not return the glove.

And then, at the very apogee of emotional strain, when one must speak or die, act or collapse – de Toth spun around and stormed out of the room.

We blinked and breathed and stirred from the waking dream in which we'd found ourselves.

Sandy spoke for us all. "What in the name of God was *that* about?"

Holding it by its index finger, Marcel shook the glove the young man had abandoned so precipitately, and –

Bank notes fell to the carpet. Marcel stooped over to pick them up. "What was the amount missing, Madame Lee?"

"Six hundred francs, Monsieur."

Marcel counted the notes, placing each one carefully on the end table. We watched the notes piled up. "One hundred . . . two hundred . . . three hundred . . . four hundred . . . five hundred . . . and six hundred francs, it is, Madame."

"Had it all along, the insolent pup," Sandy said. "I'd like to give him the thrashing of his life."

"How did you know he had the money?" Mrs. Lee asked.

"I wouldn't go so far as to say I *knew*," Marcel said. "I thought it likely, based on his behavior."

"How do you mean?" Beatrice said.

"It struck me as curious," Marcel said, "that, without being asked, Prince de Toth voluntarily demonstrated that his jacket, shirt and trouser pockets were empty. But when I asked him to remove his shoes, he refused. What conclusion was I to draw from that?"

"That he'd hidden the money in one of his shoes," I said.

"But he hadn't," Daisy said.

"No, he hadn't," Marcel agreed. "He didn't wish to remove his shoes and socks because he felt it was beneath his dignity. He's a very vain young man. Very proud."

"I noticed," Beatrice said.

"And a bit of thought shows that such a course of action does not serve a thief well. To remove a shoe and a sock, tuck the money away, then put the shoe and the sock back on takes time – time a thief can't spare. Therefore I didn't think that was the actual hiding place."

"Then why did you want us to search his shoes and socks?" I said.

Marcel's expression turned dark. "He spoke of matters of which he had no right to speak. I wanted to see him humiliated. I am not proud of this, but it is the truth." He adjusted his top hat. "Madame Lee has her money, and I have the recipe I need for my book. You will forgive

53

me if I leave you? My manuscript awaits – and time passes so quickly."

In the living room the festivities had swung into a wilder key. Cigarette smoke hung in a grey pall above the guests. The gramophone played one of the latest "jass" records from America, with its syncopated crash of instruments and growling vocal:

Tell me, tell me, tell me
'Bout that sweet potato rag
Tell me, tell me, tell me
'Bout that sweet potato rag…

Few if any of the guests had noticed our absence. Sandy found fresh drinks for us. "God in heaven," he sighed. "I'm glad *that's* taken care of."

"The nerve of that young fellow." Beatrice shook her head. "Unfathomable."

"How did it all start?" Daisy said.

"I'd taken Marcel to the kitchen," Beatrice said, "and left him with Anna and her recipes. On my way back to the party, Winifred came up to me, spluttering like a wet hen. She'd been robbed, she said. Something had to be done about it. Well," Beatrice sighed, "something was."

"What about Anna?" Sandy said. "How much did Marcel give her?"

"Far too much, I'm afraid."

"Marcel and his spending habits," Sandy said.

"What about them?" I said.

"Marcel's parents left him pots of money," Beatrice said. "Did you know that?"

"I know he always has enough."

"He's very nicely placed, let's put it that way. The only problem is – if one thinks of it as a problem at all – is that he's as generous with his money as he is with his feelings. He's tremendously sensitive and easily hurt. With Marcel you have to be very careful what you say and how you say it."

"He's delicate," Daisy said. "That's true."

Sandy picked up the tale. "The thing that bothers me most is that Marcel has no clue how to handle his fortune. I've told him time and again to put his money into something good and sound rather than something that merely *sounds* good."

"How do you mean?"

"Exactly that. If the name of the company is euphonious, he'll invest." Sandy shook his head in dismay. "Tanganyika Railway. Oural Oil Fields. Doubowaia Balka. Even if the company is on the verge of bankruptcy, it makes no difference to Marcel. If the name has appeal, he buys stock."

"And he tips like a madman," Beatrice said. "Guess what Marcel tips on average?"

"I'm afraid to hear."

Beatrice emphasized each word. "Three hundred percent."

"How much did he give Anna?" Sandy said. "Get it over with."

"For one recipe," Beatrice said slowly, "a week's salary."

"Lord in heaven," Sandy said.

An elegant greyhound of a man approached Sandy and Beatrice. They introduced him to Daisy and me and then excused themselves. "We have to circulate," Beatrice said, "though we'd really prefer to stay with you."

"We'll be all right," Daisy said. "Won't we, Ned?"

"I made it out of a foxhole," I said. "I tend to think we'll be okay."

"You mustn't leave without saying goodbye," Sandy said.

"We won't," Daisy said. Now – mingle."

The Shelton-Drakes moved off into the throng.

Daisy watched them go. "I wonder," she said, "if Sandy – "

Her fingers clutched my arm. Her face had gone white. She pointed across the room.

Allan Herbert had promised he'd stay away from the party. But now we watched him moving along the perimeter of the room, glancing this way and that, obviously keeping an eye out for someone.

"I can't believe it," I said, and started in his direction.

Daisy stopped me. "I'll talk to him."

"He's being foolish. We've got to get him out of here." Allan disappeared into a group clustered at the far end of the room.

"Let me," Daisy said. "I know how to talk to him." She went in search of her wayward brother.

I collected another glass of champagne and let the babble of voices wash over me. I watched the guests make their rounds, chatted desultorily with a guest or two, all the while keeping my eyes peeled for Allan and Daisy. When ten minutes had gone by with no sign of them, I figured Daisy had frog-marched Allan off the premises. I decided to reconnoiter and see if I could pick up their trail.

They weren't in the billiard room or the parlor that Beatrice used for visits with intimate friends. Nor were they in the high-ceilinged, well-stocked library. I edged through the smoky maelstrom of the living room and headed for Sandy's office on the second floor.

Sandy's office was a long and airy affair with a collection of African sculptures in large glass cases and a desk the size of Monaco. Bookshelves rose to the ceiling. The office was empty and serenely silent – the party's ruckus downstairs registered only as a faint buzzing. One lonely light burned on the desk. I opened a window. Cool night air lapped in over the sill. Thunder grumbled in the distance. I breathed in the moist air, glad of the change from the overheated rooms below, glad of the quiet – which didn't last long.

A gunshot ripped a hole in the night. For a split second I was at the front again. Another gunshot. Another glimpse of the inferno flashed orange and red in my mind.

The shots were nearby.

The hallway was dark as ink. A figure, black on black, ran toward the far staircase. There was an explosion of breath on the stairwell – a dull thud – a cry of pain. I reached the top of the stairs. Sandy lay sprawled on the second floor landing. I plunged down two steps at a time and leapt over him. Guests had gathered below, drawn by the gunshots.

"Where did he go?" I demanded.

Puzzled faces stared up at me, a sea of black tuxedos and silk and velvet gowns, silent and still as a photograph.

"Did someone just come down these stairs?" No answer came from the mute crowd. "Did anyone leave the house?" I realized I was shouting. They must have thought I'd lost my mind.

"Someone ran into the garden a minute ago," a woman in silver said. "I think."

I made for the side door. It led along a narrow walkway to the Shelton-Drakes' garden. The gate leading from the garden was ajar. No sign of anyone.

More people clustered at the foot of the stairs. I forced my way up the steps to Sandy. Blood oozed from a ragged gash above his left eye.

"What happened?"

"I heard a gunshot," he gasped. Pain contorted his features. "I started up the stairs. Someone ran into me. Knocked me off my feet. Hit my head on the handrail."

I helped him along the stairs.

"What in the name of Christ is going on?" Sandy said.

"I don't know. But we're sure as hell going to find out."

We lurched down the hall to the room – one of the guest bedrooms – where the gunshots had been fired. I felt for a light switch, found it – flicked. Nothing happened.

"Damned light's burned out."

"There's a lamp in the corner." Sandy let go of my arm and stepped into the room. He stumbled and nearly fell.

"I'll get it. Why don't you sit down?"

"I'm fine, I'm fine," Sandy said, bristling, and snapped on a table lamp.

A body, half in shadow, lay in the center of the room. Heavy-set, with a thick beard and very red lips: Harry Burke, just as Allan had described him.

Sandy switched on a second lamp.

Burke lay on his back. He'd been shot in the neck and in the chest. His shirt was soaked a vivid red. The bullet to his throat had sprayed blood across the white rug and walls. Eyes closed, Burke's breathing was labored.

"I'll call the police," Sandy said.

When he'd gone, I knelt beside Burke. "Who shot you?"

Burke stirred. He opened his eyes, head lolled to one side on the hardwood floor. His lips moved, but what he said – if anything – was unintelligible.

"Who shot you?"

With the greatest of effort, in a guttural whisper, he managed to produce one word. "*Day...Zeee....*"

I leaned in, my ear close to his mouth. "What did you say?"

Burke grimaced. Blood bubbled in his ruined throat.

"What was that? What did you say?"

Summoning the last of his powers, Burke opened his mouth: "*Daisy...*"

The floor reeled under me. The voices in my head went berserk, crying, laughing and howling. I clenched my fists and fought to remain on the face of the earth.

April 27, 1979
93 River Road
Point Pleasant, PA

In that hospital room in Deauville my sleep was fitful. I never found a restful state but floated just below the surface of consciousness, plagued by visions of fire, mud, and shredded limbs. I'd wake to Daisy smoothing my hair. I asked her once: "Why go to so much trouble?"

"Anyone with ears as big as yours," she said lightly, "needs all the help he can get in this world."

I couldn't deny the truth of what she said.

Grievously wounded, a long way from home, I was so young and so lonely. Daisy always had time to listen. I always had things to say.

I spoke of my childhood in a tiny Minnesota town, how I'd grown up as a serious and devout boy, ashamed of my body, afraid of the world, in love with words. I believed in God until cancer took my mother away, proving that no one listens to our prayers. I told Daisy how the world's vastness filled my soul on quiet summer nights when fireflies drifted beneath the feathery branches of the pines leading down to the lake. I wrote in the attic by candlelight, sweating in the summer, freezing in the winter, putting my thoughts on paper while the town slept. I read Robert Louis Stevenson and Joseph Conrad and Edgar Allan Poe and dreamed of living somewhere else – *anywhere* else.

Daisy's girlhood couldn't have been more different. Instead of cornfields stretching to the horizon, her world was composed of dilapidated brownstones fronting sooty courtyards strung with damp grey laundry. I craved the clamor and frenzy of the big city. Daisy dreamed of a place with no police whistles, no rattling elevated trains. Though our circumstances differed, we both felt the same wanderlust, the same inchoate longing for something not easily named. We had no clue what or where it would be found – but it was out there somewhere. Perhaps it was waiting in another city or another country. The search drove her the same way it drove me.

"Once my friend Beatrice and I ran away from home."

"How old were you?"

"Ten or eleven. We played hooky and went to Manhattan to see the circus. We loved the circus – the elephants especially. We thought it'd be the greatest thing in the world if we could be the girls who ride in on the elephants."

"You were ambitious kids."

"We also wanted to be trapeze artists and tightrope walkers. The circus was so exciting, so colorful, a change from the drab and respectable world we knew. Who wanted to be respectable? We wanted fun – thrills – adventures. So we made a decision: We'd join the circus. Late that night we sneaked away to the freight yard. We climbed into a boxcar and before we knew it, we were chuffing down the track, on our way."

"You were very brave young ladies."

"Not for long. The boxcar was freezing. We were filthy and hungry. This was nothing like we'd imagined. We gave up our idea of joining the circus. All we wanted was to go home. After what felt like hours the train finally stopped. We dragged the door open. We were in another freight yard. Rain was pelting down. A church bell rang in the distance –it was four o'clock in the morning.

"Beatrice said, 'Should we get out?' 'Beats staying in here,' I said. Tripping over the rails, we made our way to the station. The doors were locked. There wasn't a soul to be seen. Heavy drops of rain fell from the chestnut trees. There was nothing to do but take shelter in the boxcar. Pretty soon the train got rolling, and we rattled back into the Brooklyn freight yard just as the sun was rising. We sneaked into my house, cleaned up, had breakfast. No one knew we'd gone, and we never told."

"What they didn't know couldn't hurt them."

By the story's end, she'd changed the bandages on my legs. Other patients required her attention, but I kept her talking. I didn't want her to leave my bedside. "You did it again, didn't you? Caught another train."

"And another, and another."

"That's what I'd have done if I'd been brave enough."

"You've been plenty brave." She gathered the scissors and the bandages. "We wanted something to happen – something marvelous. So we kept sneaking back to that freight yard and climbing into trains. I knew my wish would come true someday. And finally something did. Something marvelous happened."

"What?"

"I'll tell you tomorrow," she said. "Now it's time for you to sleep and get better."

April 27, 1919
Paris, France

Sandy sagged against the door. "The police are on their way."

"Thank Christ for that."

I groped my way to a chair. The wailing demons in my mind must be locked away, the explosions stilled. I forced that shuddering world to a halt, still reeling with the shock of Burke's dying word: "Daisy."

Daisy had shot him? Daisy – a killer?

Impossible. Unimaginable. Unthinkable.

But what if she *had* killed Burke?

Someone rapped sharply on the door.

"Who is it?" Sandy called out.

"Beatrice."

Sandy opened the door a crack. Tumult poured in from the hall. Beatrice peered around Sandy's bulk. "Let me in."

I was sliding toward the abyss. My voice tightened. "Where's Daisy?"

"Here with me," Beatrice said. "For God's sake, let us in."

"Cover the body," Sandy said. I pulled a blanket off the bed and draped it over Burke's corpse. Glowering, Sandy let Beatrice and Daisy in. Curious faces filled the gap. He shut the door against them.

Daisy wrapped her arms around me. I breathed in the scent of her lavender and perfume, felt her body warm against mine, the thrum and the hum of us. *She is mine. I am hers.*

"Who is he?" Beatrice said.

"I've never seen the man before," Sandy said.

I asked Beatrice: "Have you?"

She shook her head helplessly. "No. I don't know him from Adam."

I caught Daisy's eye. "Any idea?"

"I haven't a clue."

Beatrice reached a shaky hand toward Daisy. "Would you help me to my room? I think I'm going to faint."

"Of course, darling."

Daisy led Beatrice out.

Sandy sprawled in an armchair, a handkerchief pressed to the cut above his left eye. He seemed suddenly fragile and old, his vitality sapped. "I'm feeling a bit faint myself," he said when the women were gone. "Nothing to be concerned about, though." He lowered his handkerchief. The wound had stopped bleeding. "What were you doing up here?"

"When Burke was shot?"

Sandy nodded.

"Looking for Daisy."

Sandy once again pressed the handkerchief to his wound and closed his eyes.

Five minutes later the lion's head doorknocker fell once, twice on the front door.

"That'll be the police," Sandy said with a groan. "Help me up."

As I got him out of the chair, a thought struck me. "Where were *you* headed?"

"What do you mean?"

"When you were knocked over on the stairs. Where were you going?"

He gave me a weak but roguish smile. "Keep this to yourself, will you? Beatrice would kill me if she found out, and there's been enough killing in this house for one night." He smiled again, but there was no humor in it. "Promise?"

"You have my word."

"I was on my way to the roof."

"What's on the roof?"

"Not what – *who*. I was going to meet a very lovely – and very willing – young woman."

Partygoers lingered in the hallway, hungry to hear what was going on. A group of men in dark suits and derbies stood at the top of the far staircase. The police had arrived.

"Good evening, gentlemen," Sandy called out. "I'm Alexander Shelton-Drake. This is my house." He faltered, then dropped to his knees and, easy as a sigh, sank to the floor.

Absently smoothing his closely cropped mustache, Inspector Jules Hilaire read through the notes he'd made while I'd spoken. He was a cool customer I'd dealt with before, and there was no love lost between us. But I respected him for his diligence and his integrity, and I had the feeling he – grudgingly – felt the same about me.

Without lifting his eyes from his notebook, he lit a gasper with a lighter made from a brass bullet casing. The only sounds in the room were the turning of pages and the slow, sibilant exhalation of smoke.

Outside the window, the sky was pearl grey with the barest trace of apricot at the horizon. Daylight would soon arrive. During my interview with Hilaire, I hadn't told him about Lawson Peters or my instructions to keep an eye on Allan Herbert. And I sure as hell hadn't told him about Harry Burke's dying word. I waited for the methodical Inspector to work his way back to me. Eventually it happened.

"…Monsieur Jameson?"

I turned my gaze from the window.

"One small point. Were you attending this party in an official capacity?"

"As a reporter?"

"Precisely."

"No. I was here solely as a friend."

He smiled thinly. "I wasn't aware your paper's reporters had any friends."

"I wasn't aware that the paper's reporters had any enemies."

"Life is full of surprises, is it not?" Hilaire made a note, then capped his pen. "This will do, I think." He tucked his notebook into a coat pocket. "You'll sign your statement when it's typed up?"

I nodded and got to my feet with difficulty – my left knee was aching. I'd been sitting too long and it was a chilly morning.

Hilaire noticed. "War wound?"

"How'd you know?"

"Many of your age were wounded. Which battle?"

"Cantigny."

"Monsieur Shelton-Drake tells me you were decorated for bravery."

"Lot of good it did me."

"My son was also cited for bravery."

"Where did he fight?"

"Amiens."

"I was out of it by then. That was one hell of a good battle. The Krauts took it in the neck. You must be proud of your son."

"Quite. He was decorated posthumously." Hilaire ground his cigarette out in an ashtray of hammered brass. "So, you understand, death is not a thing I take lightly. It's bad enough to lose lives for a just cause. For murder I have no tolerance whatsoever. Thank you again, Monsieur Jameson."

I did a quick search of the premises for Daisy. She wasn't in the living room or the library. She wasn't in Beatrice's parlor. Mathilde hadn't seen her. I went upstairs and rapped gently on Beatrice's door.

"Who is it?"

"Ned."

After a moment Beatrice let me in. Her eyes were red from crying. Her hair was down. She wore a cream silk dressing gown over white silk pajamas. In the hours since Burke's murder, the sophisticated society woman had vanished. I'd never seen Beatrice look so vulnerable.

"What is it, Ned?" Her voice was thick with tears.

"Do you know where Daisy is?"

"She's not with you?"

"No."

"She came to the hospital with us. After Sandy was admitted, Daisy brought me home and tucked me up. And then she left."

"Did she say where she was going?"

"I thought she was headed home."

"How's Sandy?"

"It's a concussion. He'll be in the hospital for a couple of days."

"Anything I can do?"

A ghost of the devil-may-care Beatrice showed through for a moment. "Turn back the clock. Make this awful mess disappear."

"Wish I could. But I'm no magician."

She touched my sleeve. "Thank you, Ned. You and Daisy are such good friends to us."

I had no reason to stay but I lingered anyway. In the library the green-shaded lamps had been shut off. I opened the curtains. Grey light filtered in. Body sodden with fatigue, mind racing in futile circles, I lowered myself into one of the padded armchairs.

My dearest Daisy. Where are you? And what have you done?

I'd intended to walk back to the Rue Daguerre, but when I stepped out of Sandy and Beatrice's door, there was Lawson Peter in the Citroen Type A Torpedo. He looked annoyingly rested and chipper. I accepted his offer of a ride home. He steered the vehicle through the stream of early-morning traffic, expertly dodging automobiles, horse-drawn wagons and pedestrians. The night's rainstorm had passed and soft sunlight filled the streets. The sidewalks were alive with people on their way to work, men in straw hats and light suits, women in summer dresses and cloche hats. The air was fresh, the buildings gleamed. I felt like hell.

"Good thing you're a hero," Lawson said between puffs on his thin green cigar.

"Oh yeah?"

"Hilaire would love nothing more than to pin Burke's murder on you. What's he got against you?"

"Long story."

"Aren't they all? Come on – fess up. What'd you do?"

"It's not me he hates. It's the paper."

Lawson shook his head and laughed. "I'd say you're both on his shit list. Any idea why?"

I laughed. "You remember the Boileau case?"

"The genial gent who chopped up his wife and mailed the pieces to a bunch of priests?"

"That's the one. I covered it for the paper."

Lawson groaned. "No wonder. You put him through the mill."

"He mishandled the investigation."

"Sez you."

"Sez the facts. Boileau was framed. But Hilaire couldn't see it and he prosecuted the poor gink. What happened? Guy croaks himself in his cell."

"Then the guy's brother-in-law had a crack-up and confessed. It comes back to me now." Lawson signaled for a left turn. "That explains why Hilaire wants to nail your hide to the side of a barn. He was up for a promotion. You wrecked it for him."

"*He* wrecked it."

"But you told the world."

"That's my job."

71

"You destroyed him so he'll destroy you. Makes sense. And he might do it, too."

"He's got nothing on me."

"Think about it, chum. You were right down the hall when it happened and one of the first to find the body. Men have been hanged for less."

"Circumstantial."

"Good enough for our friend the inspector." He flicked his cigar out the window. "You should have heard him. 'Any man who can kill during a war can kill during the peace.' And et cetera, ad infinitum, ad nauseum."

"He thinks I'm guilty? Okay – lock me up and throw away the key. But before you put my neck in the guillotine, tell me one thing. What's my motive?"

"Got me there. Unless there's something you're not telling me."

"I never heard of Burke till you mentioned him the other day."

"So you say."

"*You* don't suspect me, for Pete's sake."

"Nah. I think it was Allan Herbert. I know he was there, by the way. Though you didn't see fit to let me know that."

"It slipped my mind."

"Like hell it did."

"You think Allan Herbert's guilty?"

"I could be persuaded. He's the only guy at that party with a known connection to Burke."

"You going to tell Hilaire about him?"

"Hell, no. The French don't need to know about Herbert. I want him free so I can see where he goes and what he does when he goes there. I want to catch him in the act of giving our secrets away." He bit down on his cigar. "Catch him – and crush him."

As we approached the Place Denfert-Rochereau, Lawson circled around the Lion of Belfort, massive on its pedestal. We swung into the Rue Froidevaux, skirting the southern wall of the Cemetery Montparnasse.

Lawson pulled the car to a curb and produced a silver flask. He took a healthy pull. "Care for a snort?"

"I wouldn't mind," I said, and took a slug. Calvados burned its way down my throat and into my stomach. I handed the flask back.

"Herbert's a traitor, Ned. I'd like your help. I can do it without you if I have to. But I hope I don't."

"Why am I so important?"

Lawson took another snort. "If you don't want to play ball, I might start thinking you had something to do with him. Both you and the missus. Maybe all three of you are selling secrets to the Germans."

"Goddamnit." He'd brought this up before and I was sick of it. If I didn't get out of the car and away from Lawson immediately I'd kill the bastard. I swung the car door open. "Call me anything you like," I said. "But when you question my loyalty to the country I almost died for..." I stepped to the pavement.

"Take it easy, greasy," Lawson said blandly. "It was only a thought. I didn't say I believe it." He got out of the car. "The long and the short of it is want your help."

I strode away unsteadily. "And people in hell want ice water."

He caught me by the arm. I shook his hand off. "Do that again," I said, "and I'll kill you."

Lawson stepped back, hands raised. "Calm down, pal. I'm not General Ludendorff. This isn't Belleau Woods."

"Then leave me the hell alone." Nerves jangling, voices droning in my head, I kept walking. A minute later, Lawson zipped by, tapping the horn as he passed.

Lousy son-of-a-bitch...

I'm on a redwood dock in Lake Okabena, water blue as the cloudless sky. Beside me is my grandfather in a straw hat. Smoke rises from the chimney of an abandoned house on the opposite shore.

He points to the house. "They're waiting for us." He steps off the dock into the water but doesn't sink. He takes my hand and we walk across the lake to the house with the smoking chimney.

In the horse barn. The sweet stench of hay pervades the musty darkness. Lucy, a chestnut mare, neighs as I stroke her long brown muzzle. She eats a lump of sugar from my palm. She wants more. I sneak into the abandoned house beside the lake because I know there are lumps of sugar hidden in a trunk in the attic.

Under the attic's sun-hot eaves, my grandfather plays cards around a green baize table with three ancient men. Horse blankets are nailed over the windows. A fifth old man crouches under the table, growling like a dog. One of the men says, "Write your name on a piece of paper." I do. "That's good," he says. "You write very well."

Below us, Lucy kicks in her stall. My grandfather ignores her. He shuffles the deck, deals another hand. Lucy kicks again, harder. And again.

The old men pay no mind. Soon all the horses are kicking in a hollow storm of fear. The barn is on fire. As the barn burns the men play cards and the screaming horses thunder against the wooden stalls...

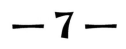

April 27, 1979
93 River Road
Point Pleasant, PA

I turned the page and found a loose sheet of onionskin paper, neatly folded in half.

…the ceaseless, or almost ceaseless, or seemingly ceaseless activity, conducted under insuperable, or almost insuperable, or seemingly insuperable circumstances. A sick man with a radiantly healthy mind…A finely upholstered cage…What rare intuition, what psychological insight! Marcel, a born detective. I can envision the story: Winter, 1910. The city is flooded. A body is found. In a submerged carriage, perhaps. A member of the aristocracy – or a beautiful dark-haired stable-boy…

This could be perhaps our strongest bond and the ultimate source of our communion: each of us has lost, or will someday lose, the one we love so desperately, so completely. I will be discovered in tears, inconsolable, left with nothing but a bouquet of memories. But even as I insist on the superiority of my grief, it will inevitably succumb to indifference and forgetfulness, just as Marcel described. The thought of losing that grief – my only tie to the vanished loved one – is intolerable. Yet grief has a life just as love has a life. Perhaps, if I am lucky, I will find my beloved dead in a time beyond time.

Someday I will die, and a phantom of myself will exist for some years in the words and thoughts of others until they themselves die. All the hours to fill till then. Like raw silk running through my hands.

Look at that. It's noon and dark as night. I think a storm is on its way…

I don't remember writing this. Then I realize with a pang that I hadn't.

Daisy wrote it after her father's death in February of 1949. Though she's writing about Marcel, her father is "the lost loved one" she will grieve for until time destroys her grief. She typed it on the Remington Streamliner I'd given her for Christmas.

She had never known her mother, who'd died shortly after her birth – one of the things that bound us together, poor motherless children caught in life's storm. Daisy's relationship with her father soured after she'd left college in 1917 to be a nurse in the War and then married me. After our return, we rarely saw him – he lived in Rye, New York with a housekeeper and a vast library of books he never read – and the few times we did were chilly, distantly cordial events. As far as I could tell, there was no love lost between Daisy and her father, and I can't say I cared for him. Poverty had hardened his heart; acquiring money had made him suspicious of everyone's motives; age had embittered him. He struck me as unloving and unlovable.

Yet his death had a cataclysmic effect on Daisy, leaving her mired in an overwhelming depression through that gray and endless winter. She lost a shocking amount of weight and stopped talking; when she wasn't sleeping, she sat listlessly staring out the window at the soot-stained apartment buildings across Second Avenue. Once so vital, she had turned into a small thing. The world we'd created together was disintegrating and I didn't know how to rescue what we had. I was confused and shocked and frightened beyond words.

But I didn't run. I didn't desert her. I held her at night just the way she'd held me in that hospital in France. I fed her. I told her I loved her – again and again and again.

I don't know how we made it through. Somehow the days passed. And, as winter slowly faded, so did Daisy's anguish. A turning point was when she laughed at some stray remark I'd made. She hadn't laughed for months. After the anguish we'd gone through, I was afraid to interpret it as a sign of a mind and a body returning to health. But that's what it was.

One bright spring morning I was eating breakfast in the kitchen. I looked up from Drew Pearson's column on current affairs, and there was Daisy at the door.

"You're up early." I spread strawberry jam on my toast.

"I haven't been to bed yet."

I was immediately worried. Sleeplessness is a sign of mania.

She placed a cleanly typed sheet of paper on the breakfast table. "Read it when you can."

78

I'd misinterpreted the signs. That morning – and what she'd written – was the start of Daisy's return to the world.

I set the fragile onionskin sheet aside. I shuffled in dew-wet slippers to the bottom of the backyard and stared out over the low hills. Though it was morning, mist still lingered in the waist-high weeds that lined the Delaware towpath.

I never much liked Arthur Lynch. I had to respect him because he was Daisy's father, and I admired the way he'd fought his way out of penury and into the upper tax brackets. Though I couldn't find it in myself to hate him, I couldn't work up any positive feeling for him, either.

But so what? I asked myself, what the hell does it matter? Arthur Lynch is long gone. I don't have to fight with him for Daisy's affection or loyalty. So why do I keep waging these old battles over again and over again? Why, when there are so many pleasant memories to lift up, to hold to the light like a crystal and examine?

Perhaps it's because anger always lives in the present moment, whereas the memories we cherish vanish in the snap of the fingers. I'm afraid I'll be subsumed by these memories, trapped in a past I can't recapture. This is the curse of growing old; the physical indignities, the mental instabilities are nothing compared to this. I see it so plainly, the past: only inches away, but unreachable.

"Ned! How goes it?"

Walter Minehart, my neighbor who owns the bed-and-breakfast down the road, strolled into view on the other side of the towpath. Walter's mother Patty was an old and precious friend of ours; she'd lived down the road from us for almost half-a-century. I was always happy to see the ever-cheerful Walt. His two pugs panted along beside him. He waved. I waved. Soon Walter and his pugs were lost behind a bend in the greenery.

It could have been any spring morning on River Road. Birds chirruped in the leafy trees. The day was warming. The sky stretched cerulean and cloudless above. The lavender Daisy planted so many years ago would soon be in bloom, filling the air with its scent and my mind with memories. This year they'll bloom without me.

The time Daisy and I spent here ran through my mind. When the house was first built, we camped out on the floor of our bedroom. The beds wouldn't be delivered until the next day, but we couldn't wait to take over our house. We woke up early the next day, a frosty morning late in the fall. The room was freezing.

"You have all the blankets," Daisy complained.

"Because I'm cold."

"Cuddle up," she said. "I'll keep you warm."

I couldn't have asked for a better introduction to the house.

That was the start of our life on River Road. All the love, all the writing that took place in that little house! And what pleasure when we returned home from a jaunt into Manhattan. I'd unlock the basement door. The scent of the house – bacon and woodsmoke – always got my pulse racing. "Hello, house," we'd call as we pounded up the stairs to the kitchen, "we're back!"

Minutes turned to hours, turned to days, turned to years, and somehow I've grown old. Why does this surprise me? Context, I think – when friends begin to die we begin to think that this life may not last forever. How can such a fearful scenario be true?

I tightened the belt of my tattered paisley robe and returned to the faded notebook and its chronicle of lost time.

— 8 —

April 27, 1919
Paris, France

Hooves pounded in my skull. I awoke bathed in sweat in the stifling sun-drenched room. I stumbled down the hall to answer the thumping on the apartment door: "Monsieur Jameson? Are you in there?"

Madame Isabelle, the building's concierge, stood beside a stocky middle-aged man wearing black livery. He seemed familiar, but I didn't know why.

"I've been knocking for five minutes," Madame Isabelle said. "I thought you were dead."

"I was sleeping."

"Hard to tell the difference," she sniffed, and held out a sheaf of telegrams. "These came while you were away. Or asleep." She waggled a crooked finger at the man. "And this gentlemen would like a word with you."

"Thank you, Madame." I took the telegrams. "Come in, please."

Madame Isabelle started down the steps. I offered the man a seat and a cup of coffee. He politely refused.

"You wanted to see me?"

"My name is Odilon Albaret," he said. "I work for Monsieur Proust."

That's where I'd seen him: in Deauville. Marcel's chauffeur, the silent figure behind the wheel of the old red Renault taxicab outside the hospital, waiting for Marcel to finish his visiting.

"Monsieur Proust has asked me to give this to you."

83

I opened the thick vellum envelope. Inside was a sheet torn from a cheap notebook. The message was written in a high, looping hand:

My dearest Ned,

Please come to see me the moment you
receive this missive. I need your help.
I hope you won't refuse this urgent
request from your old friend,

Marcel

Then I read the telegrams. There were four, and they were all from Stanley Quinn, my editor at the paper. The nicest one read:

SAW YOU IN THE NEWSPAPERS THIS MORNING
STOP TOO BAD YOU WERENT IN OURS STOP
WISH YOUD LET ME KNOW WHAT YOURE UP
TO STOP MUST SEE YOU SOONEST

I could go to the paper and face Quinn, or see what Marcel wanted. It wasn't a hard decision to make.

"I'll be ready in ten minutes," I said to Odilon.

I gave myself a quick spruce-up and left a note for Daisy on her drafting table. Madame Isabelle was sweeping the foyer as Odilon and I passed through. I gave her instructions. "If Madame Jameson returns to the flat before me, please have her telephone Monsieur Proust." Odilon jotted down the number, and twenty minutes later I arrived at 102, Boulevard Haussmann.

A raw-boned young woman in a severe black dress opened the door of the flat on second floor of the Boulevard Haussmann. I stepped from the hallway into the vestibule, followed by Odilon.

"Monsieur Jameson," he said, "allow me to introduce my wife Celeste."

Celeste was tall for a woman. Her features were striking – large brown eyes, a strong nose, a stern and sensual mouth – and her gaze was sharp; a formidable figure, far more intimidating than her stocky, good-natured husband. I knew immediately that she was a force to be reckoned with.

"You're late," she said crisply.

"The traffic was bad," Odilon said with a shrug. "I did the best I could."

"He's been waiting. You know he hates to wait."

"You'd best take Monsieur Jameson in then," Odilon said. "How is he this morning? Did he get any sleep?"

"He's had the first cup of coffee and his croissant. He didn't sleep much last night. He'll need the second cup." Celeste looked me squarely in the eye. "If you'll come with me, Monsieur Jameson."

"With pleasure, Madame," I said.

"I'll be in the kitchen," Odilon said.

He went through one doorway, whistling a bit of popular song, and Celeste and I went through another, moving ever deeper into the murky depths of the apartment.

A hallway led to a drawing room filled with furniture covered in white dust sheets. The windows were shuttered. A seep of light gave the room a subaqueous feeling, as if we were at the bottom of an aquarium. I trailed after Celeste in the near-darkness, threading my way around huge white ghosts of tables and chairs, down another hallway, darker even than the first. I quickly lost any sense of where I was or what direction I was heading. All I knew was that I mustn't lose track of my guide, the implacable Celeste.

She stopped in front of a door and knocked softly. Without waiting for a response, she opened the door and held aside a heavy velvet curtain.

The large dimly lit room was hazy with acrid-smelling smoke though no fire burned in the hearth. The windows were covered with dark-blue satin drapes, the walls and ceiling in curious squares of cork paneling. An elaborately carved oak wardrobe stood next to a Chinese cabinet thick with silver-framed photographs. Notebooks were stacked along the length of the marble mantelpiece. An ormolu clock ticked loudly in the silence.

"Good morning, Ned," said a voice in the gloom. "Or what passes for it."

A bedside lamp flicked on and I saw, in the far corner of the room, hand at the lamp switch, my old friend Marcel.

He lay propped up in bed, wearing a woolen jersey over a nightshirt.

An expensive but worn fur coat was draped over his legs. He stretched out a long white hand.

"How good it is to see you," he said as we shook. "How very good."

He turned to Celeste, who waited attentively.

"Celeste, I think more coffee is in order, if you would be so kind."

"Yes, Monsieur Proust."

"Would you like a cup?" Marcel said to me. "It's very good coffee. Celeste sees to that. You'll have a cup?"

"I will. Thank you."

"Two cups then."

The velvet curtains whispered as Celeste passed through.

"She's a marvel," Marcel said. "I count among the blessings of my life the presence of this angel named Celeste, who both sow and reaps, unlike her biblical counterparts, and make this oddly intense life of mine possible." Marcel's dark-ringed eyes glittered. "Dear Ned, please – be seated! Be seated!"

I lifted a bundle of page proofs off a velvet armchair and placed it on one of the small wicker tables beside the bed. One table was for paper, pens and ink. The second served as a place for coffee and tea. On the third table was an open pasteboard box containing a number of paper packets, a box of matches and a plate covered with powder – Legras powder, the source of the haze that filled the room. Burning the powder and inhaling its fumes helped relieve Marcel's breathing problems.

"No better?" I said. "The asthma?"

Marcel was greatly dismayed. "I fumigate myself every morning – for hours, on occasion – just to catch my breath. It is very tiresome. I can go nowhere. I am a prisoner." He smiled wistfully. "But I have come to love my cage."

Rising at four in the afternoon and retiring around eight the next morning, Marcel turned day into night. He rarely left this room, where he was engaged in a task worthy of a literary Hercules: an enormously long, enormously complicated novel. The social butterfly of his youth had metamorphosed into the dedicated middle-aged maker of literature. He'd always been a man of extremes. I admired him greatly, but found his singular focus disturbing. He wasn't taking care of himself. He ate almost nothing, subsisting on coffee and croissants; he spoke casually of using Veronal to get to sleep and adrenaline to wake himself up. How long could he sustain this taxing behavior in service of his goal?

Notebooks, manuscript pages, a plate with a few crumbs: this was the cage he'd built, furnished, and inhabited.

"*I could be bounded in a nutshell, and count myself a king of infinite space,*" I quoted.

"The melancholy Dane and I have at least that much in common. But we differ on one point. Denmark was a prison for him, whereas this room is my refuge. You would be amazed at the view I command from such limited quarters."

The velvet curtain parted and Celeste backed into the room, carrying a silver tray with a matching coffee pot. She set the tray on the table nearest the bed and poured us each a cup of coffee. Marcel thanked her, and she departed silently.

"I was delighted to see you and Daisy at Sandy's gala," Marcel said, cup in hand. "How long has it been since last we met?"

"July of '18. Just after I was discharged."

"Daisy and I saw you to the train station. How well I remember – and with such sadness – seeing you depart, headed for America. I can still picture you on the platform, thin as a twig in your army uniform, clutching your suitcase. You were very frail. I don't think I betray any confidences when I say that we doubted your survival."

Marcel was right. I was more than frail. His words reminded me of just how shaky, how damaged I'd been. I didn't want to leave France, but I was too scared to stay. My wounds had healed, but my mind was in turmoil. I was in love with Daisy, but didn't know what to do about it. I was in a spiral that could have led to my death. I don't exaggerate and I don't leave out so many of my contemporaries. The War had left us in terrible shape, whether we'd admit it or not. I did – for what good it did me.

So I ran back to Minnesota. even though I didn't want to be there. I was looking for a safe place. But there are no safe places: that's the lesson I should have learned from the War. After three unhappy months in St. Paul, I knew I had to return to Paris.

"I'm overjoyed to see you've recovered," Marcel said. "I was quite worried about you."

"I managed to keep both legs. Others weren't so lucky."

"You poor boys had the worst of it." Marcel's eyes glistened with tears. "A terrible war. Such destruction."

I thought of the hours he'd spent in the hospital at my bedside, asking me about America, my childhood, writing, plans for the future.

His curiosity was insatiable, his interest genuine. I came to depend on our daily meetings. He didn't just cheer me up. He and Daisy kept me sane.

Marcel rested his coffee cup on the coverlet. "When were you and the lovely Daisy married?"

"October 28 – just after I arrived."

"You belong here with her. Here in France. And I confess to my own selfish reasons for wishing you here. Nothing is as distressing to me as losing a friend." He contemplated the middle distance for a good fifteen seconds. "The subject of friendship is why I asked you here today. May I speak candidly?"

"Always."

"Over the years, certain of my friends have criticized my over-emotional nature. They feel that I ask too much, too soon of a friendship. They misunderstand me – as well as the nature of friendship. They claim to desire the closeness of friendship, but what they truly wish is to be the recipient of intimacies without offering any in return. No one wishes to show oneself as one really is – a naked wretch, in need of love and never finding it. They want the coin of friendship from others, but they themselves do not wish to spend a franc."

He brought the cup to his lips and drank.

"My nature is an open one. I hate to lie and have little capacity for it. But over the years I have learned to be cautious because I have encountered cruelty or – even more upsetting – disdain. I guard my heart like others guard their bank vaults. But the events of the other night force me to speak freely."

Marcel set his cup aside and adjusted the fur coat draped over his legs. "After I left the party last night, Harry Burke was murdered. I had no idea he was going to be there. I am sick with grief at the death of this man. For once, many years ago, Harry Burke was a dear friend."

The surprise must have shown on my face.

"Yes, it's true – Harry and I were once intimate friends. And by 'intimate' I do not mean to imply behavior in any way indicative of the Uranic. There was nothing illicit or shameful about the nature of our friendship." He sank back onto the pile of jerseys that served as his pillow. "I make a point of this because, once or twice in the past, similar charges have unaccountably been leveled at me. I dealt with them in the only appropriate fashion: a duel. And may I say, without assuming the mantle of the braggart, that I acquitted myself honorably." He took a speculative sip of coffee. "My friendship with Harry Burke was only of the noblest variety. It was an intimacy of souls."

Soul was not a word I'd associate with Harry Burke. Judging from his corpse, he'd been a burly fellow of sedentary habits and earthy appetites. Not to mention some illegal and highly dangerous ones.

"We met when he was spending a year abroad to perfect his French. His father was a figure in English banking circles, a Scotsman from Inverness who wanted Master Burke to have all the advantages. This was long before the turn of the century. We were barely in our twenties. He stayed on in Paris though I rarely saw him. And now poor Harry is dead and it is clear to me that I am not long for this world." Marcel's eyes closed, then fluttered open after a moment's reflection. "Would you believe that Harry once wrote poetry?"

"He didn't strike me as poetic."

"Harry was full of surprises when he and I and the universe were young. I thought his poetry showed promise." Marcel recited sonorously:

"The moon burns
Without heat
Without effect
Eaten away by oxygen
And the business of the day…"

He let the words dissolve and fade like the moon in the poem.

"The newspapers say you found Burke's body."

I started to speak, then stopped.

"I shall be as silent as the tomb." Marcel placed a hand on his heart. "I swear it. You may tell me anything. It will remain our secret. I have a good reason for asking."

Could I tell him what happened the night Burke was killed — and how Daisy might have figured into it? Keeping this a secret was ripping me apart. Marcel's large dark eyes were focused intently on me. He wanted to help — and I sure as hell needed it.

"Early yesterday morning," I said, "I was caught in one of my dreams…"

89

Marcel studied the ceiling, running long white fingers over his unshaven chin. "You're positive Harry identified Daisy?"

"I'm sure of it."

He leveled his gaze at me. "Do you think Daisy killed Harry Burke?"

"She couldn't have."

"And yet his last word is her first name. Have you told anyone this?"

"Only you."

"I am honored by your trust." He adjusted the pile of jerseys, then leaned back. "You have no idea where she is?"

"The last I saw of her was when she helped Beatrice out of the room where Burke had been killed. I have no idea where she is right now or what's she doing."

"What do you plan to do?"

"Find out figure who murdered Burke and get Daisy off the hook."

"I should like to help you."

"Marcel," I said, "I appreciate your offer. But you must take care of yourself."

"My strength may be limited, but my will is vast. That counts far more than mere animal energy. You need have no fears on my account."

I did have fears, but I kept them to myself. His overwhelming dedication to his book, his questionable health, and his topsy-turvy hours ruled him out as a partner in crime-solving.

"I have certain connections which might prove helpful," Marcel said. "I spent many years as a man of the world. In the course of my peregrinations I met figures from all walks of life, some of whom may be of use in a situation like this."

He was a persuasive speaker, capable of selling hymnals to Satan. I couldn't match his loquacity or his passion, so I buttoned my lip to wait him out.

"As a reporter, you possess an open-sesame to any number of spheres. You have the newspaper's files at your beck and call. We are well-placed, my dearest Ned, to find the killer." He clapped his hands. "Good. Now – if you'll leave me for the moment, I shall make my ablutions and dress for the day. Then Odilon will drive us to your newspaper so we may inspect the pertinent files."

"That's not a good idea." The thought of facing Quinn with Marcel in tow...

"Not another word until I'm dressed."

90

I perched on a shrouded loveseat in another dim room packed to the ceiling with furniture. Marcel shouldn't spend his limited strength searching for Burke's killer. He should be writing. He wasn't a detective. Neither was I, though I did have certain advantages as a newsman, as Marcel had pointed out, but I didn't think much of my chances. With Marcel involved the odds were worse. What a team we'd make – an asthmatic novelist and the number-one suspect. We didn't have a chance in hell.

Marcel was dear to me – and to Daisy – but he lived in a universe that ran parallel to the rest of the world. He'd insulated himself with cork walls and shuttered windows. His bedroom was a cross between a sick room and a laboratory. It reminded me of a memory theatre, a device created by the ancients to organize and recall vast amounts of knowledge. Marcel lived in this timeless world, so close to ours but as distant as the canals of Mars. I'd be better off working by myself.

I'd have to say no.

"Monsieur Jameson?" Celeste, hands clasped at her waist, stood before me.

"Yes, Celeste."

"I wish to speak with you. Are you aware that Monsieur Proust is not well? He suffers terribly from the asthma. Every day is a struggle. Since he learned of Monsieur Burke's death, he has spoken of nothing else. Now he intends to involve himself with the murder. Never in my years here has anything like this happened. I am deeply worried. You must not let him pursue this course of action. He is so frail. I'm afraid this exploit, if carried through, will kill him."

She could have been speaking of her own child. And it struck me: Marcel wasn't merely her employer. He was her precocious, cosseted boy. And Celeste was Proust's child, in a way – or, more accurately, his creation. This young woman had come to resemble her master. Proust's grave politeness was echoed by her own. I could hear his rhythms in her speech. Celeste was wife and mother, servant and child.

"He lives here alone?"

"His father and mother died fifteen years ago. He's been here by himself ever since. His mother's death struck him especially hard. The two were inseparable. When Monsieur Proust used to travel, he sent her a half-dozen letters a day – telephoned, too, when one was installed. She wanted to know everything he saw, everything he thought. He did nothing without his mother's knowledge or approval."

"Nothing?"

Her lips tightened. "No, Monsieur – nothing."

"Are there other servants, or is it just you and Odilon?"

"There is no need for others." A note of pride entered her voice. "Everything is arranged here so he may work in peace. We see to that."

"What an uncommon life he leads."

"He is not a common man. Why should he lead a common life?"

She strode out of the room. I was left alone among the ghostly furniture.

Celeste was right: Marcel was not a common man. He was extraordinary. Insulated by illness and money, he'd carved out a place to work undisturbed, with nothing to worry about but his own needs – or the needs of his book.

Celeste's fierce dedication to him and the life he led in these Stygian rooms was also extraordinary. What must it be like, living in this bell jar? Day was transformed into night, night into day, all for the sake of words on a page. This was a chapel. Or a prison. Or both.

Finally Marcel bustled in, freshly washed and shaved but dressed in last night's rumpled formal wear. "Are you ready to depart?"

When I rose to greet him, he immediately read my reluctance.

"Celeste's been at you, hasn't she? I'm grateful for her concern. But she won't stop me. And neither will you."

"We only want what's best for you."

He looked at me gravely. "…Come with me."

We returned to his bedroom. He gently lifted a silver-framed photograph from the Chinese cabinet: a slim, delicate young man with a carnation in his boutonnière, a mustache, and masses of wavy hair.

"Who is he?"

"Harry Burke," Marcel murmured. "Many years ago…"

He set the photograph back in its place on the cabinet.

"My appearance at the Shelton-Drakes' was an anomaly," Marcel said. "I have given up society. Though it is pleasurable to see old friends, it is sometimes a shock for which I am insufficiently prepared. All too often I am saddened by the changes wrought by time. My old friends must think the same about me. 'Poor Marcel,' they must say, 'how cruelly life has treated him. How he's aged. I remember him so differently…' I call on very few people nowadays, and then only in service of my book. If it requires, as it did last evening, a fragment of culinary wisdom from Beatrice's cook, then I hunt it down. The

92

knowledge of a dress, a pair of shoes, the history of a name or of a cathedral – I seek it out. I don't expect to live much longer – no, no, don't interrupt, I'm convinced of it. No one shall tell me differently. But as long as I have the will to carry on, nothing shall get in the way of the completion of my book.

"What is this opus that so monopolizes me? A version of my life, or of one I might have lived had circumstances been different. It contains as many of the people and places that I have known and loved as I can contrive to include.

"I originally conceived of the book in two volumes, but the war changed that; paper was limited and publishers had other interests than my little story. This was a blessing in disguise, as it afforded me the opportunity to greatly enlarge the scope of the work. That's how I spent the war, laboring through lonely nights here in the Boulevard Haussmann, while you were fighting in the trenches. I couldn't participate – look at me, unable to sniff a flower without a tightening of the lungs akin to strangulation. But I could write. And I did – with unceasing passion.

"My book is a collection of stories, theories and conclusions drawn from the closest observation of men and women and the structures of society they have built and inhabit. I examine the good and the bad, the perverse and the normal – if we must even use those terms. Certain elements, as I told that woman at Sandy's party, directly concern perversion. I meant to shock her, and I succeeded. But the plight of the invert is infinitely worthy of study, simultaneously fascinating and melancholy, and I try to write about it with the greatest honesty.

"Why, if this book matters so dearly to me, would I take time to investigate the death of a man I haven't seen for thirty years?

"I am driven by a superfluity of impulses: the most tender and innocent of loves or, rather, the memory of such a love; the nostalgia that arises from the death of a deeply cherished friend; and the desire to see justice done." He gestured to the photograph. "That is the Harry Burke who was intimately bound to me. It is for that young man I put my book aside." His eyes held mine in the gloom. "You cannot refuse me. Let me be a part of your investigation."

"I'm concerned for you. If anything was to –"

He interrupted me with urgency. "You want to prove that Daisy is innocent, don't you?"

"More than anything."

"And I want to recapture my love for Harry Burke. Help me."

Celeste was icy as we left Marcel's apartment. Odilon, faithful as ever, manned the red Renault taxicab. Neither Marcel nor I said a word until we were well away from the Boulevard Haussmann.

At the paper Marcel pored over the morgue files on Harry Burke. The quality of his attention was unparalleled. He peered at each clipping, examined every photograph as if it held the answer to the riddle of the Sphinx.

Stanley Quinn, shirtsleeves rolled up, suspenders dangling, poked his head into the room.

"Goddamnit, Ned," he growled, "where the hell have you been?"

I tried to answer, but he ran right over me.

"No. I take that back. I *know* where you've been. What I want is my exclusive story."

"I'm fine," I said equably. "And how are you?"

"Don't give me any guff. I want your first-person account of the Burke murder on my desk in twenty minutes. Throw in some horse radish about how badly the cops are handling the matter. It's an outrage, a scandal. You know what I'm after."

"You'll have it in twenty minutes."

"I'd better." Quinn spit a brown stream of tobacco juice into a spittoon near my foot. "Or you can forget about coming to work tomorrow."

"Curious fellow," Marcel said when Quinn had gone. "I take it he's the editor of this newspaper?"

"He's the ringmaster of this zoo. Find anything?"

Marcel tapped a folder. "There's not a great deal here. When Harry was young, he viewed banking as a profession for philistines. It was the Bohemian life or nothing. In those days his sole concern was the soul of man. Evidently his interests changed." He pushed the folder toward me. "His career in business astounds me."

Burke had long been a resident of Paris, so the clippings went back for years. Burke married, divorced, formed an investment company with a well-heeled clientele drawn from the upper echelons of the business and artistic milieus. He'd traveled a great deal, collected antiquities and curiosities, and that was all the clippings revealed.

I closed the folder. "Not very promising."

94

"Yet not completely discouraging. The newspapers – yours among them – hunger for crimes of passion. But far more people are killed for money than for love. There may be something in Harry's business dealings that led to murder. I shall make certain discreet inquiries."

"Who will you ask?"

"Lionel Hauser, a banker friend of mine. I'm sure he'll be happy to help an old chum. Tell me – do you think there's anything in the files about Allan Herbert?"

I searched the newspaper's morgue. There were a number of Herberts, but no Allan.

"It was worth a try," Marcel said, preparing to leave. "I shall approach Lionel while you write your article for the redoubtable Mr. Quinn."

"Let me know what you dig up."

"Celeste will telephone you. She may be angry at us, but she is the epitome of the good and faithful servant."

After Marcel had gone, I rang Madame Isabelle. Was Madame Jameson at home? No. Had she called and left a message? No.

I sat at the typewriter and pounded out my article. My mind kept drifting to Daisy. Not at home. Hadn't called. Where was she? My uneasiness grew. I forced myself to keep typing. Simple declarative sentences, word after word. Subject and predicate. Who, what, when, how, and –

Where.

Where are you, my love? Where are you?

Once Stanley had my story, I tried Madame Isabelle again. No sign of Daisy. I called Beatrice. Daisy wasn't there. Beatrice said that Sandy was feeling better and would be released from the hospital in the next day or two. I left the paper around eight and slid into a booth at a nearby bistro for a meal I couldn't eat. The drinks, however, I managed to get down.

After my third scotch-and-water, I knew exactly where to find her.

The Rue du Canivet is a shoelace of a street, and Number 4 is a narrow building squeezed between a butcher's shop and a storefront filled with moldering antiques.

Allan Herbert lived in a flat on the third floor.

The lingering light of early spring filled the sky, but the Rue du Canivet was drenched in dusk. I huddled in a doorway, mind roiling with indecision, working up the courage to "just drop by."

Now or never. I walked through the darkness toward Number 4.

"Ned."

Heart thumping, I stopped in my tracks. The smallest flick of orange light – flame cupped in a hand – flared in a dark doorway across the street. As I neared, the tip of a cigar glowed orange, and I could just make out Lawson Peters.

"I was wondering when you'd show," he said in an undertone.

"What are you doing here?"

"Same thing as you, pal – keeping an eye on Herbert."

"Is he there?"

"I'm waiting to see when he shows up."

"Is Daisy there?"

"No. I've got things covered. Go home, Ned. Let me do my job."

The apartment was desolate without Daisy. My need for her was an illness. A simple cure existed – all she had to do was come home. It could happen at any moment. It could happen now.

It didn't. I rambled around the apartment, unable to settle down. I nipped at a bottle of gin, hoping it would dull my mind and let me sleep. I stretched out on the couch.

Daisy couldn't have killed Burke.

Why not? She was capable of anything. But if she hadn't, then who had? Allan Herbert?

And then it struck me. It was clear as well water. I saw what Lawson was up to.

He was trying to destroy us. He'd wanted Daisy, but she'd married me. I'd taken her away from him. This was his revenge. He was a rotten, jealous son-of-a-bitch and a bad loser. But I could dismiss his conniving without a second thought.

It wasn't as easy as dismissing Harry Burke's dying words. What I needed was proof. A note, a letter, a diary…Her journal.

It helped her make sense of her life, she told me, and she kept it religiously. I'd never once looked at it. I'd never violate her privacy in that way. Once, many years ago in Minnesota, a cousin of mine – a nosy, nasty brat of a girl– read my journal. All of my youthful agonies had been exposed. I was so angry I didn't speak to her for a year. And I stopped keeping a journal after that for a very long time. A journal's a sacred thing. It must remain inviolate.

96

But I had to know what Daisy was up to.

If I could find her journal, it might explain what's been going on, help me figure out what to do. As I searched for her journal, guilt gnawed at me. I wanted to find it – and I didn't want to find it. But I couldn't calm my suspicious mind.

It wasn't behind the books on the bookshelf. It wasn't under the mattress or hidden in her dresser. The scent of lavender rose from her lingerie drawer as I searched among the silks and satins. It wasn't under her drawing paper or on her shelf of art supplies. It wasn't in her table model Singer sewing machine. But something else was.

I lifted an envelope from deep inside the machine's innards. Inside was a postcard-sized photograph and a handwritten note: *There are more where this came from…*

The photograph – *God, no.*

Celeste let me in. Monsieur Proust had not yet returned. He might be quite a while. Would I care to wait? She brought me a cup of coffee. I drank but couldn't taste it. I sat among white-sheeted tables and chairs, listening to a clock chime the hours in a distant room.

Marcel arrived just after two in the morning, in high spirits.

"Ned! To what do I owe this pleasure?" He saw the worry on my face. "What's happened, my friend? Something has affected you terribly. Come with me. We shall talk."

I accompanied him around islands of furniture to his bedroom. He draped his tuxedo jacket over the back of a chair. "I saw my friend the banker this evening." He undid his bowtie and let it flutter to the ground. "He had some captivating information, which I shall share in due course." He removed his cufflinks. "Tell me what's wrong."

I held out the photograph. His eyebrows rose. He glanced at me, then back to the photograph.

"…It looks bad, yes – a photo of your wife with another man. Fortunately – or unfortunately – it's impossible to tell just who this man is."

"If I knew who it was, I'd break his jaw."

Marcel pushed a button near the head of his bed. "Anger serves no purpose. It distorts our judgments and blunts our sensibilities. If we are to find our way to the heart of this matter, we must remain dispassionate. How did you come into possession of this photograph?"

I told him of the insane mood that had taken hold of me and of my frantic search through the apartment for Daisy's journal.

"May I see the envelope? And the note?" Marcel put on a pair of spectacles and studied the evidence.

Celeste brought in a tray with two glasses and a bottle of Evian water. She filled our glasses, then left. Marcel was oblivious to her coming and going. He straightened up. "I recognize the handwriting."

"You do?"

"Though I hesitate to tell you. Because there's so little to judge by." He removed his spectacles. "And because I fear I'm correct. A small test is in order."

He paused for reflection in front of the Chinese cabinet. He took a letter from a drawer, another from a second, and a final letter from a third. He placed them beside the note that had been clipped to the photograph.

"Study these closely, and tell me which matches the handwriting on the note."

Marcel sipped his Evian water while I examined the letters.

At length I pointed to the third. "This one."

"You're sure?"

"Absolutely. The handwriting, the way the letters slope backwards – it's the same."

"Do you know who wrote the letter you've chosen?"

"Why should I?"

"Turn it over. You'll see the signature there."

And there at the bottom of the page was:

With love,
Your Harry

"Harry Burke sent the photograph to Daisy?"

"That is my conclusion," Marcel said. "Which leads me to another conclusion. The image is out of focus; the framing is haphazard; it was taken without the knowledge of its subjects. What does this suggest?"

"Harry Burke is blackmailing Daisy."

"And Allan Herbert. And, perhaps, others." Marcel let the photograph fall. "Harry Burke, a blackmailer. I can scarcely fathom it. It grieves me to think him capable of such a contemptible act."

We were silent for a time, each lost in thought.

An idea came to me. "The photograph is badly developed. Maybe Harry did it himself."

98

"A plausible assumption."

"He must have had a place to develop the photographs. Somewhere he could work without interruption or discovery. Where would that be?"

"His home," Marcel said. "That would be the logical place."

"You know where he lived?"

"I did once. It was somewhere near the Place Des Vosges. I haven't been there in ages."

Marcel searched the Chinese cabinet till he found an old address book. He flipped through its pages. "Aguillard – Ambrose – Amiot – Authier – Babin – Bellard – Ah, yes, here we are. Burke, Harry. Number 3, Rue du Bearn." He returned the address book to its drawer. "No doubt the police have already been to Harry's flat, but it's worth a look. We shall have to be discreet, as the hour is late. Odilon will provide us with a crowbar."

"A crowbar?"

"You don't think we can simply *walk* into Harry's flat?"

"We're going to break in?"

"Unless you know of some other way to gain entry."

As if late-night breaking and entering was a regular part of his day, Marcel calmly gathered his gloves, top hat and walking stick. Full of misgivings, I followed him down the hall, through the crepuscular rooms of furniture, to the Boulevard Haussmann.

It was closing in on three when Odilon drew the old red Renault taxicab to the curb on the north side of the Place Des Vosges. Its vaulted arcades and blue-roofed buildings of brick and stone had been abandoned for the night; the windows of the surrounding buildings were dark. Odilon opened the car door and Marcel and I climbed out. The stalwart Odilon returned to the driver's seat to await our return. Our footsteps echoed in the deserted street as we passed under a sweeping archway that led into the Rue du Béarn.

3, Rue du Béarn was an undistinguished five-story building. A weak bulb burned in the cramped foyer. Marcel surveyed the dank stone and worn tiles by the light of a pocket torch, then shone its beam on the stairway. Moving as quietly as the wooden steps allowed, we proceeded to the third floor.

A metal holder containing a card marked "H. Burke" was fastened to the door on the right. I knocked…waited…knocked again. No response. I looked at Marcel, who nodded, and then I gave the door a short, sharp kick. We had no need of the crowbar Odilon had given us; the flimsy lock snapped and the door slammed against an interior wall. We ducked inside and shut the door, listening for any sign that we'd been heard.

The building was as quiet as Père Lachaise on a snowy winter night.

Marcel found a light switch. A dusty chandelier missing most of its bulbs provided weak illumination. A narrow hall led into one large room, a portion of which was curtained off for a sleeping area. A small stove and sink occupied one corner. A shoddy wardrobe stood against one wall. Bookshelves lined the others. I reached for a random volume: *Dombey and Son*, by Charles Dickens. Its pages were uncut; no one had ever read it. I checked another book, and then a third; they were also unread.

Marcel paced, hands behind his back, studying the room intently. I followed him into the flat's miniscule bathroom, where he inspected the medicine cabinet above the sink. Dentifrice, hair oil, scissors and comb. None of the items had ever been used. I trailed after Marcel into the main room where he stood deep in thought. I waited and watched. Marcel turned in a slow half-circle, surveying the shabby surroundings.

"This room," he said. "I don't like it."

"It's ghastly."

"That's neither here nor there. Something else perplexes me. Every room makes a statement, tells a story. But this room..." Marcel clenched and unclenched a gloved fist as he searched for the right words. "This room is lying. But what it's lying *about* I simply can't comprehend. There's only one thing to do at a time like this."

"What's that?"

"Go to the Ritz," he said, as if such a conclusion was patently obvious. "Some freshly steamed asparagus is just what we need to replenish our wits."

Marcel nibbled delicately at a stalk of crisp asparagus. "Marvelous," he said. "Neither under nor overdone. It's all I can force myself to eat these days." He set the stalk down and sipped from a glass of mineral water.

We sat in a small private dining room. A much-loved presence at the Ritz – his tips were as generous here as they were at Sandy and Beatrice's – Marcel virtually had a passkey to the hotel, as well as the loyalty of its staff. I toyed with a cup of coffee.

He put his glass down and, after a long, silent stretch of contemplation, Marcel said: "Tell me if I'm mistaken," he said. "Doesn't Burke's flat strike you as misleading?"

"You said the room was lying."

"Lying, yes. Or *hiding*. It's hiding something, that room. What do you know about hiding things?"

"If you can't find something, it's well hidden. If you can, then it's not."

I fancied I could see Marcel's thoughts as he examined the situation from this angle and that, turning the question of Harry Burke's flat over and over in his mind.

Something struck me. Something I'd read. "I wonder if…"

Marcel responded instantly. "If what?"

"That story by Chesterton. One of the Father Brown stories. In it, the question is asked: Where does a wise man hide a pebble?"

Marcel's eyes lit up. "On a beach."

"Precisely. Then another question is raised: where does a wise man hide a leaf?"

Marcel pondered this. "…In a forest?"

"Yes – but what does a wise man do if there is no forest?"

Marcel leaned forward, breathless and intrigued as a child. "What?"

"He grows a forest to hide the leaf."

"You've reminded me," Marcel said excitedly, "of that scintillating tale by your fellow countryman, the unfortunate Edgar Allan Poe. It also deals with how best to hide a thing. Do you know the story to which I refer? You must."

"I haven't read Poe in years."

"The story I'm thinking of is called 'The Purloined Letter.' It involves a stolen missive that everyone is searching for –" He stopped suddenly, closed his eyes, and lowered his head in thought.

"I remember it now. The letter they're looking for –"

An outstretched hand cut my sentence off. "*Please.*"

A minute went by as we sat motionless. Then Marcel opened his eyes. "Forgive my rudeness. I was pursuing a train of thought and I had to follow it."

"Where did it lead you?"

"To Harry Burke's flat. Or should I say: his *real* flat."

We made our way back to that dismal room in the Rue du Béarn.

Marcel gestured at the musty furnishings. "Earlier I said that every room has a story to tell. So I ask you: What does this room say?"

The stained wallpaper, the dusty furniture, the cobwebs hanging in the corners said nothing to me. "That Burke never cleans the place?"

"Despite the clothes, the books, the furnishings, it lacks a human presence. No one *lives* here. The unread books, the unused products in the toilet are proof of that."

"Then where does Burke live?"

"This is where Monsieur Poe enters the picture."

"'The Purloined Letter?'"

"What is that story's device? Do you recall?"

"A letter's hidden in plain sight and no one sees it because it's too obvious."

"If it works with a letter," Marcel said, "why not a flat?"

"Now I'm *completely* lost."

"What if this flat is nothing but a sham? A decoy meant to fool the hunter, divert him from the real target? Very handy for a blackmailer, yes?"

"Yes." I was starting to understand Marcel's thinking. "If this flat is a fake…"

Marcel's eyes blazed. "Then where is the *real* one? Think of Monsieur Poe, and the answer will come to you as it came to me."

"…It should be hidden in plain sight."

"Not *quite* in plain sight," Marcel said. "But the principle is the same."

He studied the bookshelf, then ran a gloved finger along the books – across the shelves – and along the juncture of shelf and wall.

"It has to be here," he muttered as he worked. "It's the interior wall so…"

With a sudden *click* the bookcase swung open on hidden hinges.

I was astounded. "This is something out of *A Thousand and One Nights*."

Marcel gave me a wry look. "Poe will do." He reached into the room and flicked a light switch. "Follow me."

We entered the crudely constructed passageway.

I shut the bookshelf behind us. Light from the naked bulb burned brightly in the closed space. Marcel examined the opposite wall and pushed. The wall swung open to reveal…

Another room.

"And now," Marcel said, "we step through the looking glass."

In the near-darkness the smell of sandalwood was strong. Marcel pressed a button and a crystal chandelier burst into brilliant shards of light. Hints of gold and silver glimmered throughout the room.

Marcel bowed with a flourish. "Welcome to Harry Burke's real home."

We'd left a dusty rat trap and entered a jewel case overflowing with glittering treasures. Pharaonic busts surveyed the centuries from fluted pedestals. Oil paintings dark with age hung on flocked wallpaper. Green-velvet horsehair sofas faced each other in front of a grand fireplace. Between the sofas a low marble-topped table featured an array of magazines and books. A quick glance revealed the expensive – and illicit – nature of the material: pornography to suit all tastes.

Here was Harry Burke's true abode, a cross between a gentlemen's club and a pasha's harem.

The bedroom walls were watered silk. White sheets, monogrammed with Burke's initials in magenta, covered a round oversized bed. In a niche was a life-size sculpture in the contemporary style. It depicted a man and woman in the throes of coitus...or an ostrich and a vulture engaged in a fight to the death – I wasn't sure which. Having glimpsed Burke's nature, it could have been either.

Down the hall was a guest bedroom. Like Burke's, it was fitted out for erotic revelry. Along the walls ran a frieze of Roman youths engaged in highly gymnastic couplings.

Marcel lifted an astonished eyebrow. "Ambitious, aren't they?"

"This place is *astounding*."

"What better place to hide a flat than inside another? Who would have guessed that Burke's false home was merely a portal to his real one?"

In a room off Burke's office I discovered a photographic lab, with its red light and trays of evil-smelling chemicals. Marcel was sifting through a well-organized desk when I returned.

"Find anything?"

Marcel gestured at the desk's pigeonholes. "Checkbooks, banking records, ink bottles, nibs, stationery – and this." He pointed at the leather-bound ledger open before him. "This ledger contains a list of initials followed by an amount of money, sometimes francs, sometimes pounds, sometimes dollars, followed by a date and year."

"A record of Burke's blackmail activities."

Marcel flipped through the ledger. The payments went back years. In some instances, a payment history was marked "closed."

Marcel indicated one of the "closed" accounts. "You see these initials?"

I squinted at the entry written in rust-colored ink. "R.S.G."

"They stand for Raoul Stephane Guerlain."

"How do you know?"

"December third of last year," Marcel said. "The day Raoul killed himself was the day this account was closed."

"You knew him?"

"For a good many years. I appreciated his loving temperament and sweet soul. His suicide shocked us all. At the time no one understood why he'd done it. Now I do."

"I remember that," I said. "It was in all the papers."

"Raoul spent his considerable inheritance and was working his way through his wife's. He pawned her jewelry, sold her dresses." He tapped the ledger. "This explains where the money went."

"Why was Burke blackmailing him?"

"Rumor has it Raoul possessed certain sexual eccentricities. Burke discovered his secrets, bled him dry, and drove him to suicide."

"Is Allan in there?"

"He's here. Along with far too many others." Marcel pushed the ledger away.

A large filing cabinet contained the substance of Burke's blackmail records. I located Allan's file: two photographic negatives and copies of the letters Burke had sent to him.

The first negative was the photo of Allan and Roy.

The second was of the government document Allan had stolen and lent to Burke. I tucked it into a pocket. I'd give it to Allan so he could return it to its proper file at the Embassy.

Marcel removed an armful of files and took them to the bathroom, where he dropped them into the large black marble tub. I did the same and soon the filing cabinet was empty. I added Burke's ledger and the letters and negatives from Allan's file to the mound of papers. Marcel opened a box of wooden matches he'd found in the kitchen.

"I've seen and heard many things in my life," he said quietly. "I'm not easily disgusted. But *this* disgusts me. Not because of what the records contain, the actions of their subjects – no. Appetite is merely appetite, neither good nor bad, and must be sated. What sickens me is

104

the merciless way in which Harry used these records. The fear he created, the pain he caused is unimaginable."

He scraped a match along the side of the box. It flared into flame and he let it fall into the tub. The fire grew in intensity. Smoke billowed, catching in our throats and burning our eyes. When the papers and photos were nothing but ash, Marcel turned to me. "Come, Ned. Let us leave this circle of hell."

As the bookcase swung open into Burke's sham apartment, we heard the hollow tread of feet on the hardwood floor.

I reached the entrance in the space of a breath. A figure hurtled down the unlit stairs. I plunged after it and hit the Rue du Foin, breathing hard. A slash of moonlight caught a man racing toward the Place Des Vosges. I barreled after him. He heard me coming up fast, turned to look – and stumbled into a heap. I took him by the lapels, hauled him to his feet, and frog-marched him back to Burke's flat. He protested meekly all the way.

Marcel got to his feet when I brought our fugitive in. I threw the man into a chair. His suit jacket was torn, his hat dented, blood seeped from a scrape on his chin.

"Who is this?" Marcel asked.

Our captive was a man in late-middle age with a corona of white hair, basset hound eyes, and a dolorous expression – Albrecht Schneider, the silverware manufacturer I'd met at Sandy and Beatrice's party. I told Proust who he was.

"Herr Schneider," Marcel said, "what were you doing in this flat?"

"I have done nothing that is wrong," Schneider said, voice tremulous.

"My good sir, I never said you did. All I asked is what you were doing here."

"I might ask you the same," Schneider said, mustering what little defiance he possessed.

Marcel turned to me. "Awaken the concierge and telephone the police."

Schneider's eyes narrowed. "You won't call them, I think."

"Oh? And why not?"

Schneider wilted. "You – you'd have to tell them what you are yourself doing here."

"On the whole, Herr Schneider, it strikes me that you have more reason to fear the police than we do. Go on, Ned."

"You won't do it," Schneider said shakily.

"Be right back," I said.

I was at the threshold of the apartment when Schneider said: "Stop. Stop. Stop."

Marcel was solicitous. "You wish to speak?"

Schneider wiped his face with a large white handkerchief. "I seem to have no choice."

"You're being quite wise." Marcel smiled. "Now, please: what brought you here?"

"I came in search of my life," Schneider said, twisting his handkerchief into an anguished knot. "I am an Austrian – a former enemy. I killed a man once. In a camp for alien nationals during the war. An accident, but who would believe me?"

"Burke was blackmailing you?"

"Yes. And all the time he wanted more and more and more. I would have to steal from my company. I couldn't do that. So I came to have it out with this monster. I came here to kill...or be killed."

"Your trip was in vain," Marcel said. "Harry Burke was shot to death last night."

Schneider's water blue eyes widened. "This is true?"

"I saw the body," I said. "You must have left the party before the murder happened."

"Then I am – free." Tears welled in Schneider's eyes. "*Gott in Himmel.* I am free."

"Please see Herr Schneider to the street," Marcel said.

"You are letting me go?" Schneider said incredulously.

"Nothing is served by detaining you any longer. Be on your way."

Schneider's relief was enormous, and he babbled his thanks as I accompanied him out of the building. I watched him scurry through the moonlight toward the Place Des Vosges.

Upon my return I found Marcel in the main room, chin on his chest, deep in thought.

"Are you sure we should have let him go?"

"He's a scared rabbit, not a murderer. Anyone can see that. I'm afraid we must look elsewhere for Burke's killer."

I was ready to go but Marcel remained wrapped in thought.

"In my book," he said at length, "the reader's perception of a particular individual is often altered by an unexpected twist of circumstance – a chance encounter, an overheard assignation, some private act accidentally made public. The scales fall from our eyes and we see that person in an entirely different light. We wonder how we could have been so completely *wrong* about someone we imagined we knew. It is often a bitter experience. The taste is of wormwood and gall." He drew out a handkerchief, a spot of white in the darkened room, and dabbed his eyes. "I ask myself – which was the real Harry: the sensitive young poet who captured my heart…or this filthy – blackmailing – *stranger?*

"Perhaps I'm asking the wrong question. The poet and the stranger both existed, so both were real. Perhaps the question is, 'How does the demon win out over the angel in the fight for a soul?' I can't comprehend it, Ned. I simply cannot understand how the young man I loved turned into the hateful destroyer who occupied these rooms. I am at a complete loss."

Halfway to the car, I stopped.
"You go on," I said to Marcel. "I'll be right back."
I found the gold pocket watch in a bedroom dresser along with other pieces of jewelry. I thought Allan would like to have the watch back. I knew Daisy would.
I found something else in my search: A rectangular velvet case. I opened it. Light glinted off a syringe resting next to a length of cord and an ornate spoon. The late tenant of these rooms had possessed a taste for heroin…and the money such a habit requires. I told Marcel.
"That explains a great deal," he said, and was silent for the rest of the trip.

Odilon eased the old red Renault to the curb on a side street not far from my building. Before we parted ways for the night, I asked Marcel: "How did you figure out that Burke had two flats?"
"You were there," Marcel said listlessly. "You were presented with the identical situation, the same facts."
"Yes, but I didn't find that secret passageway."
"How does one choose one word over another when composing a poem or a newspaper article?"
"That's no answer."
"It may be the only one I can adduce. It's a question of inclination and sensibility, as it is in so many things. My book, for instance. At one point I needed to describe the branches of a hawthorn tree. Odilon

drove me to the countryside. He broke off several branches and held them up to the car window. My asthma made it impossible for me to leave the car, from rolling down the window to touch the leaves and savor their smell. I had to content myself by feeding upon what I could *see*. But what I can see is never enough. Asthma has deprived me of the free and unlimited use of my senses. I must augment with imagination what I cannot touch, what I cannot smell, what I cannot taste or feel for fear of that infernal tightening of the lungs. I must *extrapolate*. I am predisposed to the art of detection by illness.

"What I do as an artist is not so very different from what I do when I discovered that room within a room. I am compelled to seek what is hidden. This fascination with what is hidden is not limited to literature alone, but naturally includes the full range of human behavior – the brutal and the beautiful, the sacred and the profane; the feelings inspired by a gothic cathedral and those inspired by the muscled calves of the second footman; nothing is out of bounds; all subjects, emotions, locations are equally worthy of the closest scrutiny. The artist searches for what is hidden in himself and, therefore, what is hidden in others."

Odilon opened the door me for me. As I got out, Marcel asked me: "Has Daisy ever disappointed you?"

It struck me as an odd question. Disappointed me? No. Hurt and angered me, yes. I'd done the same to her. Learning to live with each other had its challenges; we're both strong-willed people. Our temperaments clashed more than once, but we'd always forgiven each other.

I couldn't imagine life without Daisy. I'd been raised in loneliness, schooled in it by my stern and distant father. I'd mastered the art of solitude. I knew a lot about books but nothing about people. I was considered arrogant and aloof. I exulted in my eccentricities. I courted the hatred of my peers, then wondered why I was disliked. I was smarter than they were, I'd read more, and I wasn't going to let myself rot away in that tiny unsophisticated town – and I let them know it.

Army life had been a jolt. The edges were knocked off me quick. I was surprised to find that I got along with my comrades-in-arms. I could hold my liquor and play a decent game of cards. I took the Lord's name in vain often and with pleasure. Inside I was ice; that hadn't changed. Lawson Peters called me a clean-living lad, and he was right. I didn't frequent whorehouses or trade army rations for sex the way he and the other soldiers had. It wasn't from a lack of desire. I was afraid of women and disease and God's wrath. It's how I was raised. I was trapped in the amber of my past.

Daisy changed that. She broke through my reserve by not acknowledging it. I gave myself to her entirely, and she freed me from the prison of my youth. Having tasted freedom I couldn't return to such isolation.

What if I discovered Daisy was guilty of murder? Would I hide the truth? Would I tell the authorities? Would I let them know about Allan and about Burke's circle of blackmail?

Too many questions for an exhausted man who only wanted to crawl into bed.

Madame Isabelle, clutching her threadbare robe to her withered neck, grey hair braided and coiled atop her head, called to me as I passed her first-floor flat. "Monsieur Jameson, you're just in time. There's someone on the telephone."

I squeezed through the doorway and into the overcrowded junk shop that was her flat and took the receiver from her.

"Told you I'm being followed." The caller was drunk and slurring. "I gave him the slip. Come and get me. I need you."

"Who are you calling?"

The caller got truculent. "Listen, Daisy. Wait – no. Who's this? You're not Daisy."

I had a brainstorm. "I'll bring her over. What's your address?"

"…Don't know."

"Ask someone."

His receiver clattered on the floor. "Where am I?" Laughter in the background.

"…Rue De l'Arcade."

"What number?"

"*What number?*" he yelled. After a moment he said, "Number 11."

"Stay there and I'll –"

The line went dead.

"Monsieur Jameson?" Madame Isabelle was sunk in the depths of her armchair. A sleepy cat lay in her lap. "These late night calls must stop."

"Beg your pardon?"

"That young man calls whenever he feels like it, day or night, asking for Madame Jameson. I know he's her brother, but he wakes me up."

"I'll make him stop. Sorry you were disturbed."

Daisy wasn't home. I shrugged on my overcoat and slipped a pint of brandy into a breast pocket. The night air was cold. I could use all the warmth I could get.

I hailed a taxicab at the Place Denfort-Rochereau. We sped north along the Boulevard Raspail, over the Seine, past the Place Vendome to the north side of La Madeleine. I paid the fare and paced rapidly through the empty streets toward the Rue de l'Arcade, swigging brandy as I went.

I hid in the shadows of the building across the street from number 11. Black letters ran across the grey stone façade: HOTEL MARIGNY. I polished off the brandy and set the empty bottle on the pavement. The night was as still as a painting – until the hotel doors opened in an eruption noise and two revelers – yellow streetlight accenting their hat brims and the collars of their overcoats – stumbled out of the building. They bellowed a song as they tottered arm in arm along the street. Lusty, drunken voices bounced off cold stone:

Auprès de ma blonde,
Qu'il fait bon, fait bon, fait bon,
Auprès de ma blonde,
Qu'il fait bon dormir...

A cascade of raucous laughter, and they were gone. Above the rooftops a church bell somewhere tolled the hour: four in the morning.

I wobbled across the street to the hotel entrance and leaned against the building until my balance steadied. I tried the door. It opened without a sound.

I blundered into a murky courtyard lined with potted plants and bushes. The stink of garbage – rotten fish, eggshells, decaying vegetables – suffused the darkness. A shallow set of stairs led to a glass door painted with words no longer legible.

A feeble bulb lit the foyer. A scarred desk guarded an archway covered with water-stained curtains. I lifted a brass bell and shook it. The bell's clapper had been replaced with a large iron bolt. After a minute I heard slippers slapping on carpet.

An unhealthy-looking man in dark wool trousers and a grimy white collarless shirt parted the curtains. His skin was the color of mushrooms. He clutched a glass of wine in one bony hand.

110

"Good evening, kind sir," he said. "What can I do for a gentleman such as yourself on a night such as this?"

"You the manager?"

"And owner. Le Cuziat's the name. I am honored by your presence in my humble establishment. How may I help you?"

"There's a young man I'm looking for."

"I have no doubt." He bared his coffee-colored teeth in a grin. "Does this young fellow have a name?"

"Allan Herbert."

"Herbert…" Le Cuziat tapped his chin with a nicotine-stained finger.

"He's an American."

"Of course. The American – like yourself." He squinted at me in the vague light. "You *are* an American, aren't you?"

"Yes."

"I have an ear," Le Cuziat said proudly. "I can always tell where somebody's from. I take no credit for it. It's simply a gift I have, like some people have perfect pitch. During the War –"

"Is he here?"

My interruption hurt him, and he sulked. "Somewhere. Yes."

"Get him."

"If you insist. It may take me a moment or two to retrieve him. You may even have to wait." His hospitality returned. "Is there anything I can do to make your time here more diverting?"

"Just get him."

His face was downcast. "I feel I've failed when I can't provide a gentleman with something to occupy him. Is there really nothing you'd care for? Glass of wine? Newspaper? Bowl of cashews?"

I shook my head.

"Very good." The curtains closed behind him.

As the minutes inched along, my impatience grew. The room was too warm, my collar too tight. The courtyard's rancid smell seeped into the building and made my stomach heave. Every second lasted an hour. I couldn't wait any longer. I pushed my way through the velvet curtains and into the hallway beyond.

A red bulb burned in the gloom. I passed door after door with tarnished metal numbers shining faintly in the crimson light. The smell of saltwater and rotting wood filled my nostrils. I wanted to vomit.

Another hallway led me deeper. The near-darkness disoriented me

111

as I moved down its length. I reached out to steady myself and my fingers brushed against something on the surface of the wall — something circular.

A metal disc the size of a silver dollar was loosely nailed to the wall. I nudged it and it moved. Behind the metal disc was a peephole. I pressed my eye to it.

A man lay in bed, covers pulled to his chin. Marcel. A young man entered my field of vision. Very slowly he unbuttoned and removed his shirt, undid the buttons of his trousers and let them fall to the floor. He stepped out of the trousers and stood there, naked, motionless, as Marcel gazed at him.

I let the metal disc drop back into place.

I lurched down the hallway, tripping on the warped floorboards. I found another metal disk, slid it aside, peered through.

And the world exploded
Like a shell at the front

I remember pounding on the door to the room. Throwing myself against it

My voice bouncing off filthy plaster walls
Hands grabbing at me
Other voices
Swinging fists

A shining flower of pain blooming in my brain...

I shifted on the bed — if it *was* a bed — and the pain began. I was a livid mass of pain, from skull to mouth to the agony of ribs, back, legs. Panic dug into me. *My legs. I've hurt my legs.* I was back in the trenches. Maybe I'd never left. Maybe I'm lying there still, spattered with pulverized flesh, waiting for someone to find me.

Or am I in the hospital? *Please be the hospital.* I tried to speak. My lips cracked and I could taste fresh blood. *Help me. I can't speak. Can you hear me? Daisy, are you there?*

"I'm here," a voice said. "I'm here." The scent of lavender was close beside me. My fear melted and I slept.

When I woke again, our bedroom was brilliant with sunlight and I was parched with thirst. Someone had removed my jacket, shirt and shoes. My undershirt was stained with blood, my trousers torn and grimy. I'd been beaten so severely it hurt to breath. I reeled to the kitchen and drank glass after glass of water. I gingerly lowered myself onto a chair by the window. On the street below passersby moved along the Rue Daguerre, oblivious to my misery.

Where had I been – and what happened? Then it all flooded back.

The inky hallway on the Rue de l'Arcade where, fueled with brandy, fired with rage, I forced my way into the room where Daisy was making love with a stranger.

I retched into the kitchen sink and kept on retching till my stomach was empty. I sank to my knees, my aching forehead pressed against the cool tile of the kitchen floor.

I remembered being carried through Le Cuziat's building into the courtyard for a beating, then tossed into an alley.

How had I made it home? I vaguely recalled being lugged through the night air, or – driven. Yes, driven. Odilon and Marcel. They'd brought me home.

I was alone in the flat. Head throbbing, hands trembling, every muscle throbbing with pain, I tried to hide from the shame and disgust I felt for myself and for the world. It couldn't be done. It drove me to my feet and down the stairs and along the Rue Daguerre.

Bloodied and disheveled, I ignored the stares from the crowd on the Quai des Orfèvres. I brushed aside the lackeys who dotted the route to the office of Inspector Jules Hilaire. He opened his mouth to speak – but shut it at the sight of the pathetic figure standing before him. He tapped a cigarette out of a pack. "Monsieur Jameson," he said imperturbably, "you wish to see me?"

My voice was a rusty hinge. "I know who killed Harry Burke."

"Indeed?" Hilaire flipped to a clean page in his notebook. "You wish to make a confession?"

"Of a kind."

"Where would you like to start?"

I was poised at the edge of the void. I could turn back. I could easily step away.

I knew what I was doing. I hated myself for it, but I couldn't stop. I flung Harry Burke's photograph of Daisy kissing a strange man onto his desk.

"With this."

April 27, 1979
93 River Road
Point Pleasant, PA

I'm here, she said. *I'm here.*

I don't know now – I didn't know then – if Daisy had really been with me in the bedroom that morning so many years ago. I'd heard her voice, felt her hand in mine. It might have been real. It might have been a fantasy. After all this time, I don't remember. There's so much I no longer remember. But I can never forget what I did that day.

I often told my daughter Annabelle, when she was a girl, that she had to learn to give herself the benefit of the doubt, just as she did with others – a lesson I wish I'd learned myself. There's no punishment so inescapable, so unrelenting as self-punishment.

In January of 1968, Daisy was diagnosed with cancer of the bone marrow. Six months later, she was gone. She'd fallen off the edge of the world, and I couldn't catch her.

One spring weekend I rushed her to the Doylestown Hospital when pain brought her to her knees. They'd given her powerful painkillers that – for a while, at least – kept it at bay. I read in a nearby chair while she dozed. After a while she stirred. I glanced up from the page to find she was watching me.

"Can I get you anything?"

Her voice was a tired whisper. "I love you. Do you know that?"

"I've long suspected it," I said with a smile.

"Through the roof. To the sky."

117

I closed my book. "I love you, beautiful heart."

Simple words, yes, but they carried the weight of years. We'd said them to each other a hundred thousand times before. They meant so much now.

"I saw myself in a mirror the other day," she said.

"You did?"

Pain had carved deep lines around her mouth. Her skull was prominent under the pale-blue, drum-tight skin. She'd been so lovely. Though cancer had hollowed her and doused the light in her eyes, she was still lovely. The thought of her, the sound of her name affected me as deeply as it had when we were first married and living in our tiny flat in Paris.

But looking into those death-haunted eyes, I knew the end was approaching.

"I can't believe how awful I looked." Her tone was surprisingly light. "These purple bags under my eyes. My father used to say, if I hadn't got enough rest, 'The blackbirds kissed your eyes.'"

When I thought she'd fallen asleep I returned to my book. But she wasn't finished.

"You know what it took?" she said. "To come back?"

I didn't look up from my book. "Come back?"

"To you."

The moment I'd dreaded had come.

Many years ago I made it a rule never to ask uncomfortable questions. The decision I'd made as a boy was understandable; it insulated me from the unbearable heat of emotions I couldn't control. I spent a lifetime writing my way out of the cage I'd built for myself, and thought I'd achieved it. The ratcheting fear Daisy's question unleashed made me wonder if I'd succeeded after all.

I closed my book and looked into her eyes.

There was only one thing to do. It was time to break that rule I'd clung to for so many years. I took her hands in mine and said:

"What did it take? Tell me."

"Everything. It took everything."

"I deserved to lose you."

"You did."

The words spilled out of me. "I thought I'd lost you for good. I've hated myself for years. If I could go back in time, change it…"

"But you can't."

"I know that."

"We're still here, Ned. You and me. For now, at least."

A spasm of pain gripped her.

"Is it bad?"

Eyes shut tight, she nodded. I rang for a nurse, who took one look at Daisy and arranged for morphine.

"Beatniks have crazy visions on this stuff," she said after a while. "They see the Devil. They see God. They see the universe in all its majesty. Guess what it does to me."

"Turns you into a hophead?"

She laughed. "Into Snoopy. One shot and I'm on that doghouse, flying after the Red Baron." She laughed again. "No kidding," she said. "That's what happens sometimes…" I thought she might be drifting off, but then she asked, all levity gone from her voice: "Why didn't you ask? About Allan. About what happened at Sandy and Beatrice's. You could have asked."

"I was afraid."

"That I might be guilty?"

"Yes."

"Why couldn't you trust me?"

"I couldn't trust myself."

"So you turned me in. You put me in that jail, that stone room, where they all came…a woman dressed in blood…the sobbing bird that cried all night… please, I said… quiet, I said, please…then she went away…just disappeared…goodbye…"

Her voice faded. I listened to her breathe.

"…Should I go?"

"No," she said, returning from wherever the morphine had carried her. "Stay."

"I'm glad you came back."

"I didn't think I could live with you again, not after how you'd treated me. But I'd made a – a commitment I wasn't going to break."

"I thought it was because you loved me."

"Don't be stupid. Of course I love you. I always will."

"Always and all ways."

"You were on the verge of collapse. A train sinking into the sea…The inside of the outside of a cardboard box…"

I leaned forward to hear her.

"…That's why I came home. – Would you ever fix my pillow? I want to sleep for a while. Can't let this morphine go to waste."

I adjusted her pillow and straightened her covers.

119

She touched my cheek. "It's all been for you, Neddy. Everything. All for you."

When visiting hours drew to a close, I stood beside the bed. Her eyes were closed, her breathing shallow. This might be the last time I saw her. Sometime tonight the telephone might ring with the news I didn't want to hear. I fought to keep from crying. No luck. Blinded with tears, I wept silently – I didn't want to wake her.

When I'd pulled myself together, I put on my hat and walked quietly to the door. I stopped at the sound of my name.

"Yes, darling?"

"If there was ever any question of a debt," Daisy said, "it's been paid in full."

Over the last eleven years I've often thought about her words. The comfort I'd found in them was slowly replaced by ambiguity. Whose debt was she speaking of? Hers? Mine? What debt could she have to repay? Any debt was on my side. And yet...

I left the hospital that night. Ate dinner at home, tomato soup and toast. Took three bites and couldn't continue. Poured the soup down the drain and put the toast on the windowsill for the birds. Rinsed the bowl and put it back on the shelf.

I awoke just before daylight with words running through my mind. I went to my desk and uncapped my fountain pen.

When errant chemistry
Takes you from me,
How shall I fill the empty moments
Between one visit and the next?

Obdurate, inevitable,
The seconds somehow slip away.
I return to the prison of circumstance.
We hold hands in a locked room,
And wait for the turn of a key.

And then, finally, it came: that early morning telephone call. 4:32 AM. I knew what it meant; there's no such thing as a good telephone call at that hour.

120

The numbing fatigue seemed to last an eternity. Every waking moment dragged me back to the fact that Daisy was no longer here. That she would never be here again. All the hoping-against-hope fantasies, secret midnight wishes, desperate deals offered to a non-existent God...none of it's worth a damn. None of it would bring her back. It never would and it never will.

Eventually time – that thief, that healer – eases the pain. The wound is no longer so raw. There even came a day when I could think of and talk about Daisy without crying, without enduring the deepest kind of melancholy. Even though it felt like betrayal.

Like treason.

— 10 —

Hilaire found Daisy at Sandy and Beatrice's. The three friends were finishing a late lunch in the garden when the police appeared. Daisy was taken in for questioning. She answered no questions, made no statements, refused to speak, and was placed under arrest.

Later that day Beatrice stormed into our apartment. "She's your wife, Ned. How could you have done this? They've locked her up, and it's you who put her there. You've got to get her out."

I stared at the worn planks of the kitchen floor. All I wanted was to be left alone.

"Don't just sit there." Beatrice's eyes were stormy with righteous fury. "You make me so mad I could slap you."

I didn't care what she did. I didn't care what anyone did. A thought crossed my mind. "How's Sandy?"

She was taken aback. "Sandy? He's fine. The doctor says he can leave the hospital soon." She dug in her bag and brought out an onyx cigarette case and a gold-and-onyx lighter. Her hands shook as she lit the cigarette. "I'm disgusted with you." She exhaled a cloud of angry smoke. "If you won't do something, I will."

"Do whatever you like."

Her furious footsteps hammered down the stairs to the street. I uncorked a second bottle of brandy. I let my mind wander. Light shifted over the course of the day and before I knew it the sun had set and night had come.

Peering out the window of my room in that Minnesota residential hotel, I saw the postman approaching. I raced down the steps to the foyer and waited in anguish as Mr. Rust sorted through his mailbag. There must be a letter from Daisy. I yearned to see her handwriting and the *Republique Française* stamps on the envelope. After several centuries had passed, Mr. Rust held out not one – not two – but three letters. "Someone must be fond of you," he said, and went about his appointed rounds. I shuffled them until the postmarks were in chronological order, then opened the first letter right there at the foot of the stairs. "My dearest Ned," she wrote,

> *Today a letter!* Your *letter. There inside, an image*
> *of you – terribly serious indeed. And so – oh! So*
> *gorgeous. Your college days. If we'd known*
> *each other then, we'd have found pleasure every-*
> *where and you would only and always be thrum-*
> *ming with happiness. How beautiful you are. I*
> *can't wait to kiss and kiss you. You sent me this*
> *secret lovely picture at precisely the right time.*

Standing at the railing of the ship as it neared Le Havre, I watched the lights of France. The sea and sky were black with night. The ocean breeze bit into me. I turned my coat collar up and pulled my hat brim down. Somewhere on that shore, Daisy waited for me. I was boiling inside like a kettle, veins fizzing with longing and love. The boat couldn't move fast enough.

I charged down the gangplank and into her arms. We were married on October 28, 1918, and spent the first weeks of our life as man and wife in bed. We'd hold hands and talk, kiss, and make love again. Everything on earth was made to delight us. We devoured each other, we held each other, laughed and cried and whispered to each other. "Tell me something you've never told anyone before. Tell me another. Tell me more." We only ventured out for coffee, a bottle of wine, a quick meal to replenish our strength. People on the street looked strange – they didn't know our secret world.

Sitting in the bar of the Ritz, we celebrated the arrival of a check from America. *The American Magazine* had bought a story of mine about a doughboy who helps two French kids find their lost dog. When I'd written it in Saint Paul I'd given it an unhappy ending; the dog was never found. I rewrote it in Paris because I was happy. Not every story had to end in despair. That was the miraculous lesson of life with Daisy.

We held up our glasses.

"To love and writing," I said.

"To love and writing," Daisy said. "To us."

Good news kept on coming. I sold more stories. Daisy sold illustrations to fashion magazines. We'd stroll through the Tuileries on a sunny Sunday morning, Daisy in a pale yellow frock, me in my best suit, the brown tweed one, without a care in the world. The treetops shook in the breeze and sunlight danced on the grass. Music drifted from a café on the Rue de Rivoli and the scent of lilacs filled the air. We stopped to watch a juggler toss his Indian clubs at the sky. His ease and skill were marvelous to witness. I wanted to do with words what he did with his clubs. I told this to Daisy.

"Go ahead," she said.

"All right," I said. "I think I will."

"Bet you can't catch me," she said, and pelted off down the footpath.

I dashed after her with laughter on my lips and love in my heart.

Early on a morning in May, I'm at our kitchen table. The room was filled with light; no need for the gas lamps, so I turn them off. I'm exhausted but happy. Seized by an idea at three in the morning, I'd no choice but to get out of bed. I flip through the pages, catching a sentence here and a sentence there: *Pauline, at the library door, was lovelier than ever, with her honey-colored hair swept up in a French twist, exposing the line of her long white neck, bare but for a thin chain of silver. "I'm so pleased you could come," she said.*

Daisy, in my paisley bathrobe, stands in the doorway. "I woke up and you weren't there," she says. "Is everything all right?"

"Just finished a new story."

She pours herself a cup of lukewarm coffee, brings it to the table. "Read it to me."

The second telegram:

SINCE NO RESPONSE TO FIRST TELEGRAM ASSUME
YOU ARE DEAD OR OTHERWISE EMPLOYED STOP
AT ANY RATE YOU ARE FIRED STOP BEST REGARDS
YOUR FORMER BOSS STANLEY QUINN

"You look like ten miles of bad road. Are you having some kind of breakdown?" Lawson Peters, too damned breezy for his own good, grinned at me. I held the door against him.

"Go away."

"Open up, Sunny Jim." Lawson forced his way in and lifted the kitchen window. "Place smells like a brewery." Flies buzzed in the sink around unwashed plates. "Christ, kid, you look as lousy as this apartment. Get your hat."

"I'm not going anywhere."

"Wrong, bub. We're going to that joint down the street for steak and potatoes au gratin. You can't drink away your day."

At the bistro we settled into a banquette. I hadn't realized how hungry I was and devoured everything put in front of me. After dinner, Lawson lit up one of his thin green cigars. "Lieutenant Jameson," he said, "you're a prize-winning jackass. You marry the best-looking, kindest woman in the world, and what do you do? Throw her to the wolves. If I thought I had a chance in hell, I'd take her away from you."

"You can have her."

"You're dumber than I thought." Lawson poured himself a glass of red wine. "Thank God you've got friends who give a damn."

"Such as?"

"Such as me. Beatrice Shelton-Drake, for another. She's hired a lawyer friend of her husband's to represent Daisy. This legal beagle thinks the charges will be dropped. I think he's right. I've been talking – unofficially, of course – with Hilaire. This case against your wife is pretty shaky. All they've got is that photograph. It might spell blackmail, but it doesn't necessarily spell murder."

I splashed wine into my glass.

"Easy on the red eye, chief."

"Anything else?"

"That's where things stand at the moment. Hilaire is chewing nails and shitting rivets 'cause his main suspect will waltz out of jail, and there's not a thing he can do about it. Beatrice says Daisy was with her at the time of Burke's murder."

128

"Hilaire believes that?"

"Tough to prove otherwise. Sounds like things were kind of crazy when Burke got popped." He lifted the wine glass to his mouth. "Oh – something else."

"Just a font of information, aren't you?"

"That's the Ned I know. You sarcastic bastard. Must be feeling better." He sipped his wine. "No one's found the murder weapon. Add it all up and the case against Daisy falls apart like a pair of French army boots."

Outside the bistro, I thanked him for dinner and started away.

"I meant what I said, pal." Lawson was uncharacteristically serious. "If I had a chance of winning Daisy back, I wouldn't hesitate, not for a second."

"You never had her."

"Never had her to lose, either. As far as I can see, you're right on the edge of it. If she comes back you'd better get on your knees and thank the living Lord."

I couldn't face the empty flat. I had a drink or two at a place on the Rue du Bac. The workmen at the bar didn't like my company. I didn't care much for it either, so I moved along. I spent some time watching houseboats drift along the Seine. Smoke unfurled from their chimneys, curling into nothing. A painter friend lived and worked in one of those houseboats. I thought about paying a visit, but that was more energy than I could muster. I wound my way home through the twisting streets of the Latin Quarter, feeling sorry for myself. This is what had become of my youthful dreams. Alone and racked with guilt in a strange city where no one and nothing was mine. I hated where I'd come from and I couldn't stand it here. I'd no idea what tomorrow might bring. I couldn't imagine a future and I had no confidence there'd even be a next second.

Since I was a boy, I'd often found myself in this dark place, fighting a paralyzing sadness. I thought of Robert Burton's *Anatomy of Melancholy*, which I pored over in the public library: "...how many sudden accidents may procure thy ruin, what a small tenure of happiness thou hast in this life, how weak and silly a creature thou art."

Best to get home before the depths of the Seine grew too enticing.

The old red Renault taxicab was parked around the corner from my building; Marcel sat in the back. Odilon assisted him out of the car.

"I haven't seen you in days," Marcel said. "You've been neglecting me."

"I'm not worth seeing."

"Nonsense." He linked an arm in mine and we began a slow promenade. "Tell me what you've learned."

"All right, but don't tell me what a fool I am. Too many people have been doing that lately."

"Perhaps they're right to chastise you."

"I'm a dolt, but I won't admit it."

"Beatrice says you haven't visited Daisy. Wise of you, given that you're the one responsible for her imprisonment."

"They're going to release her."

Marcel slowed to a halt. "Where did you hear that?"

I told him about my conversation with Lawson, and this pleased him. "Marvelous. What will you do when she's free?"

"Ask her to forgive me."

We proceeded toward the Place Denfort-Rochereau as dusk fell. A lighted streetcar throttled past automobiles and pedestrians. The activity in the Place, the lights and the people brought me out of myself. It had the same effect on Marcel; he was observing the life of his native city — the source and subject of his book. In the center of the Place, the Lion of Belfort kept majestic watch over the quarter. His strength reminded me of Daisy, the determined, leonine guardian of my life — until I betrayed her.

Marcel interrupted my dispiriting thoughts. "You caused quite a fuss the other night," he said casually. "Le Cuziat was all for having you arrested."

"Who?"

"The gentleman who owns the establishment from which you were forcibly ejected."

The episode washed over me in a hot flush of regret. "I'm still sore from that beating. You took me home?"

"Odilon and I, yes."

"Thank you. I was wondering."

"I can't say I know Le Cuziat well. When I was gathering material for a certain section of my book a friend of mine suggested I speak with him. Le Cuziat proved to be a very helpful source. He telephoned me when you got into trouble."

Why would he call Marcel? There was no need to. Marcel had

been with a young man in one of the rooms of Le Cuziat's brothel.

Marcel continued: "I was dining with a friend who lives near the Rue de l'Arcade. I'd left the number with Celeste. She gave it to Le Cuziat, who called to ask for my advice on the matter. You'd mentioned my name, evidently."

Now it was clear. Marcel was delicately probing to see how much I remembered. He was telling the story he wanted me to believe, waiting for me to contradict him. That evening was a source of shame for me and, if he wanted to forget it, too, I was happy to oblige him.

"I don't remember much of anything about that night. And I despise what I *do* remember. If Le Cuziat said I mentioned you, I guess I must have."

"He called," Marcel went on, "and Odilon and I made sure you got home safely."

We turned right on the Rue Boulard. As if by magic, the old red Renault taxicab waited at the corner, the stoic Odilon behind the wheel.

"So – Daisy will be set free," Marcel said. "We must redouble our efforts to find Harry's killer."

"I've no idea what to do."

"Our only recourse is to wait and watch. What we must do will reveal itself. I wish you all luck with Daisy," he added as we reached the Red Renault.

I'll need more than luck, I said to myself. *I'll need a Goddamned miracle.*

"I had a word with Jules Hilaire," Marcel continued. "He's an old school friend, you know. He kept Daisy's arrest out of the newspapers as a favor to me. He wasn't easy to convince, but I'll wager he's glad now that the case against Daisy is evaporating."

The last thing Daisy needed was to have her name in the papers, identified as the main suspect in a murder. She was strong but she wasn't impervious. It would have devastated her – and torn our marriage apart.

Although I might just have taken care of that myself.

I thanked Marcel and started toward home.

"A last word of advice, Ned."

I stopped. "Yes?"

"Daisy's tired of that pedestal."

"What pedestal?"

"The one you've placed her on. That's the trouble with pedestals – the air is clear, but there's little room to move. She's happier here on earth."

Odilon shut the car door and took his place behind the wheel. I watched them drive away.

On the walk home, I thought about our conversation. Had I put Daisy on a pedestal? I loved her and depended on her, but had I turned her into a statue? I didn't think so, but no one would describe my judgment as infallible these days.

Someone had slipped an envelope under the door of our flat. *No address, no name — it's got to be from Daisy.* I opened it with nervous fingers. I took out the note and read:

> *Ned,*
> *Will you please come to 4, Rue du*
> *Canivet? I'd like to talk. It's*
> *about Daisy.*
> *Allan*

I trudged up the threadbare carpeting to the third floor. The flat on the left side of the landing had a rectangle of paper thumbtacked to its door. Written in an elegant hand in purple ink: *Allan Herbert.*

I rapped at the door.

"Ned." Allan, in grey flannel trousers and an open-necked shirt, let me in. "Thank you for coming. May I get you a drink?"

"I wouldn't mind."

Allan's manner was a little too bright. He was uneasy and trying hard not to show it. He poured cheap rye into mismatched glasses and offered me one. "Cheers."

From the bile-green wallpaper to the water-stained plaster ceiling, Allan's one-room flat was a fragment of purgatory. A table nearby held a hotplate and saucepan. A wind-up gramophone sat on a crate near the window. Allan stood beside a flimsy wooden chifferobe.

"You wanted to talk?"

"I've seen Daisy."

"I haven't."

"I wouldn't bother. She doesn't want to see you."

Blood pounded behind my eyes. "I'll believe it when she says that herself."

"I understand why. She told me what the War's done to you. How you drink. How you scream at her. How violent you are when you're in one of your rages. I've heard it all."

132

I fought to keep my anger on its leash. "What I do isn't the point. It's what *she's* done."

"And just what is that?"

"She cheated on me."

"You believe that?"

"I've got a photograph." I removed the picture from my breast pocket.

Allan took a long pull of his drink. "You thought that was Daisy?"

"Of course."

"It's not her."

"No? Then who is it?"

"I was hoping it wouldn't come to this." Allan opened the chifferobe door and stepped behind it. I could hear him sorting through the chifferobe and the clinking of clothes hangers.

"Where did you find that photograph?"

"Hidden in our flat."

"And you think Burke was blackmailing Daisy because she was having an affair with someone?"

"What else should I think?"

"Burke wasn't blackmailing Daisy. He was blackmailing *me*."

The chifferobe door swung shut.

And Daisy stood before me.

A haze of sunlight filled the window behind her, illuminating her honey-colored hair and the pale yellow frock she'd worn when we'd first gone walking in the Tuileries.

She wasn't in jail – she was right here in the room.

As I looked closer the illusion vanished. Given the right circumstances, a blurred photograph of Allan dressed like his sister just might fool a troubled husband.

Allan removed the honey-colored wig. "That's me. In the photo. I was taken at a ball in Montmartre. And that was me at Le Cuziat's place on the Rue de l'Arcade. Roy met me there. We needed to see each other. It was the only safe place I could think of."

I sank onto the sofa. "...I'm a fool."

"Yes, you are," Allan said simply. He closed the chifferobe door. He'd removed and hung up the wig and the frock. "I've decided to trust you about something else. I hope I won't regret it."

"You can trust me," I said – and meant it.

"Colonel Horatio Case. Know who he is?"

"The man behind President Wilson. The power behind this Peace Conference."

"On the Colonel's orders, I was instructed to leak information to the German delegates at the Conference – *faulty* information."

"Why?"

"To destabilize them. And the English and the French, for that matter. Now before you say, 'They're our Allies, we're in this together,' let me tell you – we're not. Wilson's head is in the clouds. England and France will divide Europe between them. They'll take it all, like greedy dogs. Colonel Case won't let that happen."

"Burke was your conduit to the Germans?"

"That's right. At first, things went as planned. Then Burke discovered my secret and put the screws on me. If the Embassy found out, my career would be over; the Colonel would have to deny any knowledge of what I'd been up to. Burke had me. I gave him every cent I had, whatever I could borrow, whatever I could sell. But you know all about that. I'd have told you the rest but I was sworn to secrecy. Not even that horrible Lawson Peters person knows about it." He took my glass and refilled it. "I said I wanted to kill Burke, but I didn't do it. Daisy talked me out of it at the party. I came home and got blotto." Just like now. Speaking of which..." He refilled his glass with several fingers of rye, then knocked it back. "...She's a good kid, Daisy. I'd go see her."

"You said she doesn't want to see me."

He reached for the rye. "Change her mind."

By the time I reached the Rue Daguerre I was worn out and starving. The air in the apartment was stuffy. The place was deadly still. I opened the window and heard the occasional voices of pedestrians below. I ran a hot bath and soaked my battered body. I scrambled a few eggs and cooked some bacon, drank a glass of red wine, washed up the dishes, tried to read: all of it meaningless motion without Daisy.

I'd made up my mind. First thing in the morning, I'd go see her.

What would I say? I lay in the darkness, rehearsing what I might say. Speaking words at the cracked ceiling. I didn't want to live like this. It reminded me too much of my Minnesota boyhood when I was afraid I'd never escape, never find love.

I thought of Allan and Roy. I hoped they'd find someplace where they'd be happy.

I thought of Marcel in that squalid room on the Rue de l'Arcade.

Daisy and I knew that Marcel was an invert. We weren't naïve and we weren't bothered by it. The other elements of his life were arranged to his liking – or to the promptings of necessity, which may well be the same thing, so this must be what he wanted. He lived in a dimly lit cave, surrounded by millions of words, a record of the life he'd lived and then abandoned to turn into fiction. Money allowed him to do as he pleased. It must be nice. Or maybe it wasn't. Money has its own problems. Or so I've heard.

I miss you, my dearest. Sometime after midnight, I slept.

At dawn, I bathed and shaved and duded myself up. Somehow we'd figure things out. She'd forgive me and we'd start anew. If she was willing.

To hell with the cost – I took a taxicab to the Prefecture of Police on the Île de la Cité. I hurried under the massive dirty-yellow archway and down echoing marble hallways into the heart of the building. I asked to see Madame Julia Jameson.

I'm sorry, Monsieur. According to our records, Madame Jameson was released this morning on the orders of Inspector Hilaire.

Where did she go?

I have no way of knowing, Monsieur. – Next, please.

I pounded on the Sandy and Beatrice's door until Mathilde appeared.

"Is Mrs. Jameson here?"

"She was earlier, Monsieur. She may be at the hospital with Madame. Monsieur Shelton-Drake comes home today, you know. If you'd like to leave a message –"

I ran back to my taxi. "American Hospital. Quick."

A nurse directed me to Sandy's room. I scurried past porters, nurses, patients and doctors, and paused in the doorway of room 127.

Sandy was propped up in bed. Marcel, hands clasped around his walking stick, was perched in a nearby chair. They broke off their conversation when they saw me.

"Ned," Sandy said. "Here to spring me, are you?"

Marcel touched the brim of his top hat. "Good morning." His complexion was chalk white and the rings under his eyes were darker than ever. He looked dreadful. I thought of what Celeste had said: he was a man of great will but inconstant strength.

Sandy was wan, worn, and his good humor seemed forced. "Heard the news? I'm headed home today. Damned doctors. It's all nonsense. Clear off a chair and sit down."

"Where's Daisy?"

"She's been with Beatrice all morning."

"I accompanied Beatrice to the jail," Marcel said. "Once Daisy was freed, we came directly to the hospital."

"They went to the house. Once they get Daisy's room ready, Beatrice will get me out of this hell hole."

"Daisy's room?"

"She's asked to stay with us for a while," Sandy said after an uncomfortable pause. "It's nothing to worry about. After what she's been through, Daisy just wants a little time away from – from – "

"From me." I put on my hat and started for the hallway.

"Where are you going?" Sandy said.

"Wherever Daisy is."

"Don't rush things."

I came to a halt. "I've got to apologize."

"Take Sandy's advice," Marcel said. "You mustn't – "

"It's not Daisy in that photo. She wasn't being blackmailed so she had no reason to kill Burke. Someone else did it."

Marcel straightened up. "How did you find this out?"

"I spoke to – "

Beatrice lugged a suitcase into the room. When she saw me, she studiously ignored me. I understood Beatrice's cold shoulder, but didn't like it.

Beatrice plunked the suitcase on the foot of Sandy's bed and undid the latches.

"Where's that blasted doctor?" Sandy said.

"Down the hall. He'll be here soon." Her tone was as crisp as the white shirt she placed on top of a fresh union suit.

"That's all I'm waiting on," Sandy said as Beatrice carefully added a tie, argyle socks, a tweed jacket, a pair of trousers and a hat to the pile. "He flashes a light in my eyes, signs a piece of paper, and I'm a free man."

"Take that hat off the bed," I snapped. I leapt toward Sandy, but Beatrice snatched the hat away, cowering from me. Was I that frightening a figure? Is that what she thought of me now? "It's bad luck," I added, feeling awkward. "Hats on beds. That's all."

After a moment Sandy got to his feet and gathered up the pile of clothes. "I'm breaking out of this antiseptic prison," he said to Marcel. "You can get back to your book and I can get back to my affairs."

"You'll be home in less than hour," Marcel said. "Your stay in the hospital will soon be nothing but a vague, unpleasant memory."

"I hope to hell you're right." Sandy disappeared into the bathroom.

Beatrice refused to catch my eye. She latched the suitcase and set it next to the bed. "I'll get the doctor," she said, and bustled out of the room.

I gave a long whistle. "Guess I'm not on the list for her next party."

"Don't be too hard on poor Beatrice," Marcel said. "The past several days have been a severe strain. A stranger murdered in her home...Her oldest friend arrested for the crime...Is it any wonder she's upset?"

The bathroom door opened. "What are you two nattering on about?" Sandy, pulling on his jacket, sat on the bed and reached for his shoes.

"Plans and provisions," Marcel said.

A stooped figure in a white smock marched into the room. After a perfunctory examination, Doctor Santeuil said that Monsieur Shelton-Drake might leave the hospital at his convenience.

Marcel clutched my arm as we trailed after Sandy and Beatrice. It was clear he was reaching his limits. "You must rest," I said.

His voice was faint with fatigue. "Not until we've found Harry's murderer."

"But that could take weeks – months."

"On the contrary," he said. "I shall settle the matter this afternoon."

I came to a sudden halt. "You know who did it?"

"All in good time. We must proceed with caution. A trap can only be sprung once."

What trap had he set – and who would he catch? If Daisy were guilty, Marcel would have said so. He knew how my suspicions were devouring me.

Sunlight splashed across the hospital lawn, the bright spring weather contrasting sharply with my muddy thoughts. Beatrice guided Sandy into their limousine. Marcel signaled to Odilon, who drove up to the curb.

137

"Be at Sandy's by four o'clock," he said. "I believe I have properly assembled the pieces of this puzzle. It's time to let the authorities – and the world – know."

— 11 —

A thought, a line, a refrain nags at me. I can't seem to place it. It's from a poem, I know that, but which one? In the living room I opened a box of books – the ones I've decided to take with me to Amherst – and dug out the likeliest suspect, an old college textbook.

This battered volume has traveled with me from house to house, continent to continent, decade to decade. It's a beloved object, like this pen, this desk. I carried the book to the side porch, where Daisy and I often had our breakfast in good weather.

Weather. Yes. Something about the weather.

Bright spring weather. That's the phrase I used in the old notebook. But where did it come from?

Flipping through the textbook, I found it. A stanza from Thomas Hardy's "The Going":

> *Why, then, latterly did we not speak,*
> *Did we not think of those days long dead,*
> *And ere your vanishing strive to seek*
> *That time's renewal? We might have said,*
> *"In this bright spring weather*
> *We'll visit together*
> *Those places that once we visited."*

We left France early in the spring of 1940. That time was a particular

141

horror, though nothing compared to the years of Nazi occupation. Everyone felt a dreadful anticipation. Night was about to descend and daylight might never return. The situation was made all the worse by the glorious weather. Paris had never been lovelier; the future had never looked more deadly. We sailed from Le Havre on a boat crowded with exiles. We didn't know if we'd ever return – or if there'd be anything to return to.

We settled into an apartment in the east 30s. I freelanced for *Newsweek* and wrote a novel about France that garnered some modest acclaim. Daisy worked with Carmel Snow at *Harper's Bazaar*, doing fashion illustrations and assisting with the magazine's layout. We'd meet for lunch and worry about the War and the situation in Europe. In those days the radio was always on. We were living two lives: one in Manhattan, pleasant and productive; the other in Paris, nervy and distraught.

Annabelle was born in the fall of 1940. We were old as parents go – I was 46 and Daisy was 44. Her pregnancy surprised us both; we'd assumed we were past that time in our lives, and we weren't keen on bringing a child into a world that was tearing itself apart. Annabelle might have been an accident, but she wasn't a mistake. We couldn't have asked for a better daughter.

My age and status as a family man kept me out of the draft. I wrote and edited material for the Office of War Information and the Voice of America. Jack Houseman was my boss. Under his English public school exterior, he was a shy and sweet-natured man, generous with theater tickets and bottles of scotch. One way or another, Daisy and Annabelle and I made it through the War years in suspended animation.

In the winter of 1947 we made our first trip back to Paris. Annabelle stayed with Daisy's half-sister Margot and her husband in Saratoga Springs while we spent five weeks searching for the city we'd lost.

Drab and gray as the sky above, *La Ville Lumière* hadn't recovered from Germany's barbaric occupation. That February was exceptionally harsh. Hunger and exhaustion showed on every face. We heard roosters crowing in the heart of the city; Parisians were raising poultry and other animals in their courtyards to keep from starving. Electricity and heating were erratic. Paris, once the epitome of style, was threadbare and scrawnier than a graveyard cat.

But it was good to be back, good to see old friends who'd survived the War. An old pal of mine on the Paris *Tribune* told me Lawson Peters had gone underground with the *Maquis,* the French Resistance fighters who lived and fought in the mountains. He'd spent the Occupation blowing up Nazi supply trains and helping American soldiers escape the country. He was back in the States now, working with government intelligence. None of this was surprising. Lawson always had a taste for intrigue.

Other friends hadn't been so fortunate. Stanley Quinn, my old editor, stayed on after the Nazis invaded. He'd been tortured and shot for printing anti-German propaganda. Shortly before the War, he'd married Brigitte, a young French woman, and they had a child. On one of our first nights in Paris, she invited us to dinner – mealy potatoes and grey meat. We were happy to share it with her. Her son, a big-eyed serious boy of seven, sat at table with us. His name was Edward, but he went by Ned. I asked him what he wanted to be when he grew up. "A writer," he said. "Like my father."

There was another reason for our trip. Through her work for *Harper's Bazaar,* Daisy had come to know Brendan Copeland, an editor at Simon & Schuster. He was a frequent guest at what Daisy called "our long table," a monthly gathering of writers, painters, radio actors, and magazine staffers. Brendan found our stories about pre-war Paris of great interest. When he heard we were planning our trip, he commissioned Daisy to assemble a collection of Proust's correspondence. "Ned's the writer," she protested, "Not me." Brendan wouldn't take no for answer. "I trust my instincts," he said, "and they say you're the one for this project." His instincts and a delightful advance – very helpful for passage on the Cunard Line – convinced her. Thanks to my pal Jim Agee, who worked for Henry Luce, I finagled a commission from *Fortune* for a piece on post-war France. We'd both be working on projects, ready to help each other when help was needed. Ah, that voyage! Nothing better than a trip with Daisy, packed with work and love.

We'd dropped a line to Celeste and Odilon to let them know we were coming, but received no reply. We'd heard they ran a small hotel not far from the Church St.-Sulpice. We decided to stop by on the off chance they'd be home. Daisy and I entered a run-down building on the Rue des Cannettes, rang the front desk bell, and waited.

Dressed in a hand-knitted sweater over a dowdy brown dress, Celeste emerged from a back room. "May I help you?" she said – and couldn't go on. We watched her expression shift from recognition to

143

surprise to disbelief to unrestrained joy. This stern, unemotional woman from the provinces embraced us and we all wept. Newspaper in hand, suspenders dangling, Odilon peeked through the curtains to see what the fuss was about – and soon he was crying, too.

We joined them for dinner that night. Celeste apologized for the scanty meal, but to us it was a taste of the past. *Boeuf bourguignon* and a *tarte tatin* with fresh bread and country butter, courtesy of Celeste's relatives, transported us to Paris before the War.

When the dishes had been cleared, Odilon poured each of us a skinny shot of brandy, emptying the bottle. Celeste told us Wartime stories. Odilon nodded gravely at her list of atrocities committed under the Nazi reign. He brightened as we talked about Annabelle, about America and New York.

"I am told it is a grand city," Celeste said. "Many of Monsieur Proust's friends have been there."

"Would you like to visit?" I said.

She thought about it, then shook her head. "Paris is enough."

"Do you see Marcel's friends?" Daisy asked.

"Not many. Most of them – how would you say – withered on the vine after Monsieur Proust's death."

Our conversation spun on. We talked of Marcel and the years on the Boulevard Haussmann. When Daisy mentioned the commission she'd received for a book of Marcel's correspondence, Celeste sat up straight in her wicker-backed chair.

"But this is splendid!" She rose and left the room.

I looked at Daisy. Daisy looked at me. We both looked at Odilon. He smiled, shook the last drops of brandy into our glasses, and lit his stubby pipe.

"You have been to the Radio City Hall of Music?" he said.

"Several times," Daisy said.

"If ever I went to New York, that is where I would go."

"It's something, all right," I said.

"And the Bridge to Brooklyn? It is still there?"

"Last I looked," I said.

"I would like to visit that also. I have seen pictures, of course, but to actually walk across it, over the raging waves of the East River – "

Celeste returned with a cherrywood box. "Madame Jameson, if you please."

Daisy hesitated, then raised the lid.

"Notes from Monsieur Proust," Celeste said. "Often, after a night of laboring, while he slept, I'd paste his new pages into the manuscript. He left instructions about what I should do and how I should do it."

Daisy delicately lifted a sheet of paper out of the box. "Look at this, Ned."

The sight of Marcel's inimitable looping script suffused me with a feeling of loss. I thought of his last years. In 1919 he'd been forced to leave his cork-lined room on the Boulevard Haussmann when the building was sold to a bank. Marcel had put his mother's furniture in storage and, after a prolonged and unpleasant search, he moved to the Rue de l'Amiral Hamelin. He'd been miserable there; his routine, and therefore his progress on his book, had been destroyed. His neighbors were noisy, intrusive pests; he risked asphyxiation from a faulty chimney, so he left it unlit and shivered under layer upon layer of clothing; his asthma grew worse and he had problems with his eyes. But he kept working even as his health broke and death approached.

Daisy gently placed Marcel's note in the box. "This is remarkable."

"Something else." Celeste held out a narrow cloth-bound book. "This contains the addresses of Monsieur Proust's friends. They will have the letters you seek." Beatrice accepted it as if it were the holy grail...which in a way it was. "After Monsieur Proust's death, no one cared how we felt or what we were going to do with our lives. I was just his stupid, long-suffering maid and Odilon his good-natured dunce of a chauffeur. We were not famous, we were not rich, and so they abandoned us. Everyone – except you, my little ones. Everyone but you."

At Celeste's urging, we moved into their hotel. She wouldn't hear of us staying anywhere else. We didn't *want* to stay anywhere else – not even the Ritz. They looked after us as scrupulously as they'd once looked after Marcel.

Daisy traveled throughout the city and its suburbs, interviewing people and collecting letters. I listened to shop keepers, street cleaners, firemen, and maids, taking the pulse of the French. After our working day was over, Daisy would show me the newest additions to her ever-growing trove of correspondence. To read Marcel's letters was to be in his presence – and to feel the awful weight of his absence, again and again.

145

Near the end of our trip, on a blindingly bright cold day, Daisy and I placed a bouquet of artificial flowers – all we could find in wintry Paris – on Marcel's grave.

On November 18, 1922, Robert Proust rang to let us know of Marcel's death. We hastened to the flat, where a distraught Robert led us into the bedroom. Marcel's body was covered with a white sheet. His beard and mustache were lightly flecked with grey; the circles under his closed eyes were dark as his hair. He might have been asleep, but the life force had flown. Marcel had disappeared into the notebooks on the mantelpiece, into the proofs scattered about the room. He had become his book.

After a while we thanked Marcel's brother and took our leave. In the stairwell we passed two young men, one tall and thin, dressed to the nines, the other dark and slightly built, lugging a camera and tripod. The taller of the two was Jean Cocteau. He introduced us to his friend Man Ray who, at Cocteau's request, was to photograph Marcel on his deathbed. He could tell from our expressions that we didn't think much of the idea. "He must be memorialized," Cocteau said. "And it is I who must memorialize him."

We ducked into a nondescript bar for a drink.

"Cocteau's a talented young man," I said.

"He has two great loves," Daisy added. "Himself – and posterity."

I had to laugh. Daisy laughed, too. We both needed a joke to lighten our sorrow.

Marcel's death reminded us of the passage of time, of who we'd been when we met, and who we were now that he was gone. Back then we were young enough to be more concerned with the deaths of those we loved than with our own. It never occurred to us that we would die.

We sat in that little bar and reminisced about the fascinating and eccentric creature who'd appeared one day on the hospital ward: Marcel, bearing gifts. He noticed a copy of Anatole France's *Penguin Island* on my bedside table.

"Are you reading this?" he said.

I told him I was.

"What do you think of it, young man?"

I told him it was a satire as beautiful as it was scabrous.

He brought out a small golden fountain pen and a long narrow notebook and wrote down my comment. "I'll tell Anatole you said that." He tucked the pen and notebook away. "He'll be most amused."

He came back the next day, and the next, and the next after that. He read some short pieces I'd written about my time in the trenches. He was particularly taken with a short story about growing up in Minnesota. I learned from him that what I was trying to escape – the disorder and sorrow of my childhood – was something to embrace and use in my writing. "It can be a source of strength for you," he said, "the psychic stream that drives the mill of your invention."

Marcel was right. When I delved into the radioactive material I'd avoided for so long I became a writer. With hard work, I transformed the misery of those years, the bone-chilling winters and the brain-melting summers and the endless lonely space of the prairie, into the stuff of fiction.

We attended Marcel's funeral service at the church of Saint-Pierre-de-Chaillot, along with a selection of his friends from the nobility, his dear friend and former lover Reynaldo Hahn, and Serge Diaghilev, sweating in a massive fur coat and bowler. Le Cuziat, the brothel owner, stood at the back of the church and wept. We followed the hearse to Père Lachaise and solemnly watched the casket lowered into the ground.

And here, a quarter of a century later, we stood by his grave again. Daisy read aloud from one of Marcel's letter to his old friend Georges de Lauris:

> *Now there is one thing I can tell you: you will enjoy certain pleasures you would not fathom now. When you still had your mother you often thought of the days when you would have her no longer. Now you will often think of days past when you had her. When you are used to this horrible thing that they will forever be cast into the past, then you will gently feel her revive, returning to take her place, her entire place, beside you. At the present time, this is not yet possible. Let yourself be inert, wait till the incomprehensible power... that has broken you restores you a little, I say a little, for henceforth you will always keep something broken about you. Tell yourself this, too, for it is a kind of pleasure to know that you will never love less, that you will never be consoled, that you will constantly remember more and more.*

Our second return was in the summer of 1958. Hard to believe that it took us so long. Annabelle came with us. She was exactly the perfect age – 17 – to fall in love with the city. She spent a year in Paris when she was in college and, later, got her doctorate in French literature. This led to a much longer stay in France, as well as a French husband – and, eventually, a French divorce. Bertrand shared the Gallic male's propensity for mistresses. This didn't affect Annabelle's love for the country. She knows more about France and its writers than I ever did, and she teaches French literature at Smith College. Hemingway had it exactly right. Paris is a moveable feast for the ones lucky enough to have been young there. Annabelle carries the feast of Paris with her still. And, odd as it may seem, I do too.

As we got older traveling became more difficult. Feet hurt. Hips ached. Energy flagged and the spirit of adventure faded. We thought we had the strength for one final visit to the country that had brought us together, to the city we called home for so many years.

In the winter of 1967, we sat in front of the fireplace on River Road with maps and travel guides spread out on the coffee table. Very quickly our trip grew from a week in Paris to a second week in the south of France with a side trip to London. In the end we decided on *two* weeks in Paris because Paris meant the most to us. It was the city of our hearts. We bought our tickets for the *S.S. Paris* and arranged our hotel. We'd written to our friends we'd see them soon.

That January, a routine check-up revealed Daisy's cancer. A blood test at the Doylestown Hospital showed that she had multiple myeloma – cancer of the bone marrow.

She wanted to go to Paris anyway. I wouldn't let her. We fought over it – terribly.

And we didn't go.

> *In this bright spring weather*
> *We'll visit together*
> *Those places that once we visited.*

Early in the morning of the day we'd planned to leave, I came downstairs. I peered into the living room. Daisy was already up. I stood there quietly as she tossed the travel brochures into the fire and watched our farewell to Paris go up in flames.

— 12 —

Sunlight blazed in the courtyard of the Shelton-Drakes' home on the Quai de Bourbon. I checked my pocket watch: twenty minutes to four. I lifted the lion's head and let it drop once, twice against the oak.

Mathilde led me into the living room. "Madame will be with you momentarily." Ten days before this room had pulsed with laughter and music. It felt like a lifetime ago.

Daisy was somewhere in this house. Was she lying in bed in one of Beatrice's white-on-white guest rooms, missing me?

Beatrice appeared. Her hair was up and she wore a simple, belted frock. Her manner was frosty, but at least she was speaking to me.

"Will she see me?"

"Not right now."

"She has to sometime." I forced a smile. "We're all a part of Marcel's plan."

Beatrice looked pained. "Don't mention that. Sandy's furious about the whole thing."

I followed her to the drinks table. "Why furious?"

"He's afraid Marcel will make a fool of himself." She uncapped a silver cocktail shaker. "The police haven't gotten anywhere with this, why should Marcel?" She dropped ice cubes into the shaker. "There's another reason Sandy's upset. Marcel won't leave him alone. He's on Sandy's heels wherever he goes, talking about his book. You know Sandy adores listening to Marcel go on about his writing. But not today."

Worry flickered across her face. "He should have stayed at the hospital. I should have forced him."

"Maybe you should have."

"They wouldn't put up with him one more night. Two nurses quit, and a third was ready to go. It was Sandy or the staff. I had to bring him home."

"Once Marcel's settled the Burke murder, things can return to normal."

"I don't give a damn who killed that awful man. It's Marcel I'm worried about."

"When I saw him this morning, I was struck by how ragged he is, how ghostly."

"He's on the verge of a physical breakdown. I'm think this will kill him." Beatrice set down the bottle of gin and sank listlessly onto a couch. She twisted a cigarette into her onyx holder. "Be a good sport and fix me a drink. I haven't the strength. While you're at it, shake one for yourself."

"I'll pass."

"Suit yourself." Beatrice closed her eyes and leaned into the cushions. "These last few days have been hell. I need a drink, and I don't care who knows it."

I filled the measuring glass with gin and poured it into the shaker, then added vermouth.

Beatrice held the lighter flame to the tip of her cigarette. "If things aren't bad enough, that despicable man from the police is here, too."

"Hilaire?"

"Is that his name? He's got a mustache he's very proud of."

I shook the gin and vermouth, then poured it into her glass.

Beatrice accepted it eagerly. "Mmmm. That's perfection. You mix a damned fine drink. I just might let you back into my good graces."

"How's Daisy?"

"Fine, for someone whose lug of a husband had her flung in jail on a trumped-up murder charge."

I sat down beside Beatrice. "I need to make it up to her."

"It's a little late for that."

The doorbell sounded – two short, impatient bursts.

"If I lose her, I lose everything. Won't you help me?"

A tear ran down Beatrice's cheek. She dabbed it away. "I'm doing everything I can."

Lawson Peters puffed on a thin green cigar as he gazed out over the Shelton-Drakes' garden. Albrecht Schneider perched on a chair, looking miserable.

A clock in the corner chimed four times as Beatrice rose and led us to the upstairs room where Harry Burke's life had ended. Marcel and Inspector Hilaire waited inside.

The room was close with afternoon sun. Gouts of dried blood were spattered across the white walls and carpeting. The smell clawed at my stomach.

Chairs were arranged in a semi-circle on one side of the room. Sandy was already seated, arms folded and jaw clenched. Lawson and Schneider sat near the door. Beatrice, looking pale, was next to Sandy.

I took a chair. "How are you feeling?"

"How do you *think* I feel?" Sandy growled. "I'm being forced to take part in a game of charades. This is an arrogant act of personal vanity and a colossal waste of time."

"If any other way presented itself," Marcel said, approaching, "I'd have chosen it." He moved as if each step hurt and wheezed faintly as he breathed

"Can't you stop this?" Sandy said to Hilaire. "The poor man's about to topple over."

Hilaire smoothed a thumbnail along his mustache. "I have spoken at length with Monsieur Proust, and on the basis of our conversation I am willing to listen to what he has to say."

"The inspector is an old school chum," Marcel said. "We were at the Lycée Condorcet together. He is used to hearing me ramble."

"Get on with it," Sandy grumbled.

"We await one more guest. Or should I say – two."

As if on cue, the doorbell rang below. A minute later, Mathilde ushered in Allan Herbert. He took a seat without saying a word. He was trying hard to appear relaxed, but his fingers worried his hat brim and his left foot tapped an erratic rhythm on the carpet.

"Ah – our final guest," Marcel said, turning to the door.

Daisy stood there. I thought my heart would stop.

Beatrice led her to a chair next to Allan Herbert, who pecked her cheek and murmured in her ear. Daisy sat with her hands folded in her lap, eyes downcast. She didn't seem to hear him. She wasn't in this bloodstained room; she was somewhere else. She wore a light tan dress

153

I didn't recognize – it must have been Beatrice's. Her blood-shot eyes showed she'd been crying for days. I wanted to comfort her, smooth her hair until she fell asleep in our bed on the Rue Daguerre. But she refused to acknowledge me.

"Ladies and gentlemen, welcome." Marcel paused to collect his thoughts – though I had the feeling he knew exactly what he was going say. I listened to the faint whistling sound of his breath. We waited for him to speak.

"Less than seventy-two hours ago, the Shelton-Drakes threw a party to celebrate the advent of *Seed*, a magazine dedicated to the latest in arts and letters. Many people were invited to this lavish event: contributors to the magazine; painters, poets, musicians, artists of every sensibility; critics and tastemakers; and, just for good measure, a string quartet.

"One person who was *not* invited was a man named Harry Burke. As it happens, I knew this man many years ago as a dear and beloved friend. Time, as it will, drew us apart and sent us on separate courses; the path he took led him into what Dante called a dark wood where the straight way is lost. Burke is responsible for a monumental amount of pain and suffering.

"On the night of Sandy and Beatrice's party, in this very room, Harry Burke was mortally wounded. The signs of his murder surround us, and his murderer is with us today. It is my intention to reveal the guilty party and turn him over to the authorities."

"Him?" Lawson said.

"Or her," Marcel said. "As the case may be."

"Includes the ladies," Sandy muttered. "A real gentleman."

"Please, Sandy, such remarks serve no good purpose." Marcel ran a handkerchief across his sweat-covered brow. "I should like to begin with a question for the lady of the house."

Beatrice sat up with a start. "Yes?"

"Has anyone been in this room since the night of the murder?"

"No."

"Has anything in this room been touched or moved since that night?"

"No," Beatrice said, after looking around the room. "Nothing's been touched."

"No one has been in here since the police left?"

"Not even the servants. It's been strictly off limits ever since...ever since that night."

"Ned, I ask you the same question. Has anything in this room changed since you were last here?"

"The chairs weren't here," I said, "but other than that..."

"Everything else is, as far as you can tell, the same?"

"Yes."

"Even the lighting?" Marcel addressed the others. "A small point, perhaps, but for the sake of accuracy I must ask."

Sandy grumbled something unintelligible. Marcel ignored him. "Ned?"

"The lighting hasn't changed."

Marcel pointed. "One lamp on the end table, the other on the dresser?"

"That's right."

His lips pursed in thought. "The lamps were used that night, were they not?"

"They were, yes."

"Who turned them on?"

"Sandy."

"But not the overhead light?"

"No."

"And why was that?"

"The overhead light didn't work."

"Does it work now?" Marcel turned to Hilaire. "Inspector?"

Hilaire flipped the switch. Nothing.

"Thank you." Marcel stroked his blue-stubbled chin. "Ladies and gentlemen, let us turn our thoughts back to the night of Harry Burke's murder.

"Among the multitude of guests were a number of people who had dealt with Burke in some capacity.

"Allan Herbert, a young gentleman associated with the American Embassy and the Peace Conference currently taking place in the city.

"Albrecht Schneider, an Austrian silverware manufacturer whose business is based here.

"Also present were friends of the Shelton-Drakes and of mine, Ned and Daisy Jameson."

When Marcel spoke Daisy's name, I glanced at her. Our eyes met. The intensity of her gaze caught me off guard, clouding my mind. Electric seconds passed. Then she cut me off behind a mask that hid her thoughts. I couldn't read her expression, couldn't tell if she was bored

155

or amused or threatened. I realized I knew nothing about her. Not a damned thing.

It was a harsh lesson, but I grasped it for the first time. She didn't exist because of me or for me. She was alone in this world – like me – and nothing we could do would change that.

I forced myself to concentrate on Marcel, who was introducing Lawson Peters –

"– who is also attached to the American Embassy. I understand you were not here at the time of the murder?

"That's right," Lawson said. "I was at the Embassy when Burke was shot. I've got a dozen witnesses who'll swear to that."

"We shall remove you from the category of suspect, then. Now – I spoke earlier of the separate paths Burke and I had taken in life. To my very great dismay, I learned that Burke had turned into a criminal of the lowest kind – a blackmailer. Monsieur Herbert was one of his victims. Isn't that so?"

Allan's face was blank. He might have been waiting for the Metro to arrive or a firing squad to discharge its bullets.

"Harry Burke possessed certain information that he used to blackmail this young man. The nature of this information is irrelevant. Let us allow Monsieur Herbert his privacy."

"Thank you," Allan said quietly.

"Did you see Burke that night?"

"I did not."

"But you came here to see him?"

"I came here," Allan said, "to kill him."

Marcel was unfazed. "And did you?"

"I was going to, but – Daisy stopped me."

"Where were you when Burke was shot?"

"I left before that happened."

"Thank you, Monsieur Herbert." Marcel dabbed at his brow. He was paler, if such a thing was possible, than he'd been earlier. He tucked the handkerchief away and addressed Albrecht Schneider.

"He was blackmailing you, too, was he not, Herr Schneider?"

Schneider nodded, looking more downcast than ever.

"Did you see him at the party?"

"I had…" Schneider cleared his throat and started again "I had no idea he had been here."

"You didn't kill him, then?"

"Of course not. I am not a violent man."

"Then how do you explain what happened in Handforth?"

Hilaire stopped writing in his notebook. "What is this Handforth?"

"Herr Schneider, do you wish to explain? It is, after all, part of the public record."

"Yes, I will tell." Blinking rapidly, Schneider turned around in his seat to address us. "It was what you call an internment camp. For enemy aliens. In Cheshire. I was there most of the War. One day I was attacked by someone. This man was crazy. He tried to strangle me. I pushed him away and he fell and hit his head. Three days later he died in the hospital there."

"If you killed once," Lawson said, "you could do it again."

"I was defending myself!" Schneider half-rose from his chair. "A man died, yes – but I am not a murderer." He glanced at each of us in turn, mouth working soundlessly, eyes imploring us for…understanding? Sympathy? Mercy?

Then he bolted for the door.

"Get him," Hilaire bellowed, and went after him. I wasn't far behind.

Schneider made it down the stairs and through the living room, but we caught him in the foyer, hauled him back upstairs, and threw him onto a chair.

Hilaire towered over him. "Are you ready to confess?"

"I am not the one you want," Schneider gasped.

Hilaire was implacable. "It does no good to deny it."

Schneider edged into hysteria. "It wasn't me. You must believe it. I did nothing. Nothing…." His words disintegrated into sobs.

"That was foolish of you, Herr Schneider," Marcel said. "Running away like that accomplished nothing. Why did you run?"

"I was afraid," the Austrian said in a near-whisper, sounding like the child he'd once been.

Marcel placed a gloved hand on Schneider's shoulder. "There's nothing to fear, my friend. I know you're innocent of the terrible crime that has drawn us together today." He paced to the center of the room. "Ned?"

I sat up straight.

Why were you at Daisy at the party?"

"We were invited."

"There was another reason, yes?"

I glanced at Lawson, who nodded. "Lawson Peters asked me to keep an eye on Allan Herbert and anyone he might meet there."

"Why was this?" Hilaire said.

"Government business," Lawson said sharply. "That's all you need to know."

"Where were you when heard gunshots?"

"In Sandy's office," I said. "I was looking for Daisy and Allan."

"What happened then?"

"Someone ran down the hall. It was too dark to see who. Whoever it was collided with Sandy on the stairs and knocked him for a loop. I helped him to his feet and we came here, to this room."

Marcel digested this. "And then?"

"Sandy and I found Burke lying on the rug." I pointed. "Right over there. Sandy left to call the police. Burke was still alive – barely. I knelt beside him and asked who'd shot him."

Marcel's dark eyes burned into mine. "And he said?"

"One word: *Daisy.*"

"Never," Beatrice cried. "Daisy wouldn't kill anyone."

"I didn't believe it," I said. "So I asked him again."

"And he said it again?" Marcel asked.

"Yes. Then he died."

The room was silent as Marcel mulled this over. "Extraordinary," he said softly, "quite extraordinary." He sat beside Daisy and nonchalantly asked: "Tell me, my little one, did you kill Harry Burke?"

Daisy contemplated the question, then spoke with calm assurance. "Burke was an evil man who deserved to die. But I didn't kill him. I'd never compound evil with evil."

"Nicely phrased," Marcel said. "A fine philosophical point, as well." He patted her hand. "Thank you, my dear."

"If she didn't kill him, why did Burke say her name?" Hilaire said.

Marcel jumped on Hilaire's question. "Ah, but *was* it her name?"

"Ned heard him say it. Twice." Lawson's tone was laconic. "I'd think he'd know his wife's name when he heard it."

"But consider the circumstances," Marcel said. "Burke was in great pain, his throat torn by a bullet, his life rapidly ebbing away. Ned might have misheard – misunderstood."

Lawson was having none of it. "You're just getting tricky. This dime novel stuff won't wash."

"If it wasn't *Daisy,*" I said, "what *did* he say?"

158

"What other possibilities present themselves? Burke was desperate to identify his killer. Who are the main suspects? They're here in this room. If, for the sake of argument, we exclude Daisy, we are left with Allan Herbert and Albrecht Schneider." Marcel pointed to the bloodstains on the white carpeting. "Put yourself in Burke's position. You've been shot. Death is only seconds away. How do you identify your killer?"

"You say his name," Hilaire said.

"Naturally. Even though Burke had been wounded gravely, he could still speak. Depending on who shot him, he could have said 'Allan' or 'Albrecht' or 'Herbert' or 'Schneider.' And yet –"

"He points the finger at Ned's better half," Lawson said.

So it would seem, Monsieur Lawson. There's only one problem with that interpretation of events."

"Is there?"

"There is indeed. The only problem is – and I have confirmed this with both Allan Herbert and the lady of whom we're speaking – *Harry Burke never met Daisy*. He never saw her, never heard her name. How, then, could he identify her as his killer?"

You've done it. Marcel, you've done it.

"Burke failed to name his killer, but a clue to his – or her – identity exists." Marcel held up a piece of paper. "This."

"What is it?" Lawson said.

"A fragment of notepaper found in one of the dead man's pockets. An address is written on it. I recognized it immediately as Harry Burke's handwriting."

"What's the address?" Beatrice said.

"All in good time, my dear Beatrice. First – let me ask Monsieur Herbert where he lives."

"4, Rue du Canivet," Allan said.

"And you, Herr Schneider?"

"158, Rue Montmartre."

"That's the financial district, yes? Quite near the Bourse?"

"That is so."

"And the Shelton-Drakes live here on the Quai de Bourbon."

"What does it say?" I asked. "What's the address?"

"One moment, Ned." Marcel turned to Beatrice. "You told me you'd never laid eyes on Burke until you entered this room the other night. Is that true?"

159

"It is."

"And you, Sandy? Had you ever seen Burke before you found his body?"

"This is a parlor trick," Sandy grumbled. "Rabbits out of hats and killers out of scrap paper."

"Perhaps," Marcel said agreeably. "But the question remains, and I ask you to answer it. Had you seen Harry Burke before the terrible night he was murdered?"

"Of course not."

"Then why was a piece of paper bearing your business address discovered in the dead man's vest pocket?"

"I don't understand, Sandy," Beatrice said. "Did you know Burke?"

Sandy's lips twisted with disgust. "It's bunkum. That's all this is — bunkum."

"But is it? Think again of what happened that night. Ned heard gunshots, he and Sandy came to this room, they found Harry Burke. Sandy leaves to call the police and Ned kneels beside Burke. Like this." Bracing himself with his walking stick, Marcel knelt beside the invisible corpse. "Who killed you?" He looked up, his features distorted with pain, and spoke as the dead man in a harsh whisper: *"Daaaay-zeeee…"* He repeated it, then let his head drop to simulate the moment of death. He looked up. "Is that what happened?"

"That's it, yes."

He extended a hand and I helped him to his feet.

"Now, my friend," he said, "read the address written on this bit of paper."

I took the paper. "46, Rue des Écoles."

"You see?" Marcel addressed the group. "Burke died before he finished the name of the street. All he could manage to say was '*Day-zeee…*'"

"That's a heap of work for a small return," Lawson said. "You're stretching it mighty fine."

Marcel wasn't perturbed. "You'll admit it's a possible interpretation."

"Possible, sure. But so is snow in July."

Hilaire tapped his pen impatiently on his notebook page. "So you claim that Monsieur Shelton-Drake is the guilty party?"

Sandy glared at Marcel. "I didn't kill Harry Burke. But I'm glad

160

someone did. The man was a bed bug. Whoever crushed him should be given the Legion of Honor."

Beatrice put a warning hand on his arm. He ignored her and continued, his voice gravid with outrage. "What happened is this. Burke's killer ran out of this room, knocked me down the stairs and put me in the hospital. He could have broken my neck. I could be dead now, too. And you have the gall to accuse me of murder?"

"Monsieur Proust," Hilaire said, "speculation is all well and good. But can you *prove* that Monsieur Shelton-Drake killed Monsieur Burke?"

"Things are very seldom how they appear, Inspector. We think a friend possesses one set of qualities. It turns out he is a stranger to us, unknowable and unknown. At times we are forced to view things from an unexpected angle. So it is with the murder of Harry Burke."

"Marcel was like this at this school," Hilaire said to the room. "A simple question never received a simple answer."

"Examining the circumstances of the case," Marcel continued, "one asserts and denies in sequence. What A says is true; what A says is not true. B claims thus-and-so; but what if B is lying? One looks for gaps, incongruities, the unexplained. There is one very striking unexplained factor in this case."

"Yes?" Hilaire said.

"Harry Burke was shot to death – but no gun was found."

"The killer took it with him," Sandy said, aggrieved by Marcel's rank stupidity.

Marcel thought it over. "Perhaps. But what if that's not the case? I ask myself these things, hoping that a new interpretation of events will present itself."

"If the killer didn't take the gun," I said, "what *did* he do with it? He must have hidden it."

Hilaire was dubious. "Just as I arrived on the scene, Monsieur Shelton-Drake fainted and was hospitalized. We searched this room shortly after. There was no time, no opportunity to hide the gun."

"Not much time – but enough." Marcel shifted his attention to me. "You tried turning on the overhead light, yes?"

"And it didn't work. So Sandy turned on the table lamps."

"The bulb must be broken, yes?"

"I'd assume so."

"How did it get broken? This is how. After he shot Burke, Sandy was faced with two problems: first, to hide the murder weapon; second,

161

to escape without being seen. He solved both problems with one brilliant gesture. He tossed the gun into the porcelain bowl of the overhead lamp. The gun hit the light bulb and broke the filament. That's why it doesn't work. That's why Sandy had to switch on the lamps after the murder."

"Tripe," Sandy said.

"Shall we take a look?" Marcel turned to the door and called out: "Jeanne!"

One of the maids carried in a ladder and placed it under the clouded glass bowl. Marcel hooked a heel on the bottom rung. He started to climb, then swayed and stepped back down. "Ned, will you do the honors?" I took his place.

At the top of the ladder, I surveyed the faces below, everyone watching except Daisy. I reached into the thick glass bowl, felt about – lifted something out of the light fixture – and held it up for all to see: a stubby grey handgun with a black grip, a Webley Bull Dog Revolver. I descended the ladder and placed the ugly little weapon on Marcel's outstretched palm.

Marcel approached Sandy. "I believe this is yours."

"Believe what you like."

"I've no doubt the license for this weapon will confirm my belief. The good Inspector Hilaire will investigate and –"

Sandy snatched the gun out of Marcel's hand.

"Stop!" Hilaire shouted.

Sandy pressed the gun to his temple. For a second nothing happened. Then Beatrice screamed as I hurled myself at Sandy, driving him into the wall. The revolver went off with a roar and a bullet ripped into the ceiling. Sandy and I slid to the bloodstained carpet. I knocked the gun out of his hand. My ears rang from the explosion. The smell of gunpowder burned the air.

Hilaire pounced on the murder weapon and wrapped it in a handkerchief. "I think this settles things, Monsieur Proust," he said triumphantly.

"I think not," Marcel said. "We want no loose ends, no loopholes for Sandy to squeeze through. No doubt he will claim that he was framed for Burke's murder and saw no other way out of his dilemma than to shoot himself. But when one last question is answered, Sandy's guilt will be proven beyond a doubt. That question concerns the gun. Surely you see it?"

162

The room sang with tension. It was too warm, we'd been here too long, the gunshot had frayed our nerves. None of us could answer.

"Why is the gun still in this room? Why didn't the killer come back to claim it? Why didn't he hurl it into the Seine where it would never be found?

"Because he couldn't.

"Monsieur Schneider or Monsieur Herbert could easily have contrived a reason to come to the Shelton-Drakes and, unobserved, remove the gun. Who among the suspects in this room had to bide his time because he was kept from returning to the Shelton-Drakes?

"Sandy.

"He played his part too well, you see. Attempting to direct suspicion away from himself, he took a more serious fall on the stairs than he'd intended. He hurt himself so badly he had to be hospitalized and was only released this morning. I made sure he was never alone from the moment he returned to this house and therefore had no chance to remove the gun. That's the truth of the matter, isn't it, Sandy?"

Sandy could have been carved out of stone, a ferocious Old Testament God of wrath.

"We know you did it." Marcel spoke with infinite gentleness. "There's no way around it. You murdered Harry Burke."

The light went out of Sandy's angry eyes. "You took long enough to wrap things up." And he laughed. But the laughter died in his throat.

Stanley Quinn wanted an exclusive on the Burke murder case. I wanted my job back with a substantial raise. He called me every name in the book and invented some new ones, but in the end I got the job and the raise and Stanley got his story.

Most of it.

Marcel asked to be left out of the official version. He wanted to return to his book, and Hilaire was happy to play the hero. That's how I told it and that's how it appeared on the front page of the paper. But that came later.

After Sandy's arrest Beatrice broke down completely. Dr. Spencer sedated her and ordered her to bed. Daisy wouldn't leave her friend's side. As a trained nurse, she was perfectly capable of caring for Beatrice. She'd be staying indefinitely on the Quai de Bourbon.

I didn't get a chance to talk to Daisy before I left that day.

Marcel and Odilon drove me home. It was a desolate city we motored through. Although I was relieved that Daisy was innocent, I was terrified I'd never see her again. Without her love I was no better than poor Sandy. I might as well be in prison.

Odilon found a place to park on the Rue Gassendi. Marcel shivered with exhaustion. Solving Burke's murder had been an enormous drain on his limited reserves.

"You were marvelous this afternoon," I said. "Thank you for saving Daisy."

His voice was nothing more than a whisper. "I did what I could. I'm glad some good came of it. But I also think of Harry, of what he became, and I despair. Nothing can change the destruction he caused. He deserved to die – God forgive me for saying it. And I weep for poor Sandy."

"You solved the case."

"Daisy is free. I cling to that."

Marcel was ill at ease, an unusual state for a man usually so self-possessed. I'd never seen him like this, but I knew not to force the matter. I let him take his time.

"There's something I haven't told you. In fact, I'm not sure I *should* tell you. I fear you'll think less of me." He gave me a sliver of a smile. "I've grown vain in my old age."

"I'll never think less of you for anything, Marcel."

"I shall test your statement, then. Have you asked yourself *how* I knew the gun was concealed in the light fixture?"

"You used logic."

"Once I'd found the gun, it was easy enough to figure out the details of the murder. But the gun came first."

"What do you mean?"

"I went to the Quai de Bourbon this morning so I could accompany Beatrice to the jail and then to the hospital. While I was at their house, I went into the guest bedroom for another look at the scene of the crime. Beatrice didn't know I'd been up there."

"That's when you found the gun?"

"I was reviewing the sequence of events and my attention was drawn to the bulb-that-didn't-work. It struck a curious note. I asked for a stepladder and inspected the light fixture. There was the gun. I could have told the police and left it at that, but I wanted to see this affair to its conclusion. Am I a vain and indolent poseur? Have I disappointed you?"

"You're a miracle worker."

"You are too good to me." He took my hands in his. "Until soon, my dear friend."

Odilon held the door for me. Leaning into a corner of the back seat, Marcel shut his eyes, withdrawing from the events of the past few days and preparing for his return to that room on the Boulevard Haussmann where his real work waited. He cared for Daisy and me, and he'd gone to great lengths to find Burke's killer, but we weren't essential to him. No one was, except Celeste and Odilon, who made his peculiar life possible. I could see him through the window of the old red Renault, but he'd already vanished.

Alone, rifle on my shoulder, boots silent in the snow, I plod beneath a canopy of blackened branches. I must get through the woods to the river, where a cluster of soldiers waits for me. I must reach the river before dark or I'll be left behind. I quicken my pace. From overhead a sound like gloved hands clapping. A grey barn owl flies above me. I lift my rifle, aim, and fire. The owl falls to the snow. I run to it. Blood pours from its breast. I watch it die.

I woke up, enveloped in sadness. I pulled on my clothes and left the apartment. It was four in the morning. I wandered through the sleeping city until I reached the Pont Alexandre III and gazed into the Seine until the sun was up. The urge to step off the railing had weakened; it was too much effort. I wasn't going to jump. No one would care if I did. Living or dying, it was all the same. There was nothing to do but go home. I was too sick of myself for anything else.

Daisy was there, packing a suitcase.

"Hello, Ned." Her tone was cool, amiable. "I needed some clean clothes."

I watched her slim figure as she went from drawer to suitcase and back again.

"You're going back to Bea's?"

"I am."

"How long will you stay there?"

She folded a middy blouse and laid it on top of a grey skirt. "I don't know." She closed the suitcase and fastened its hasps.

I couldn't force her to stay. It must be her choice to come back to me. I stepped aside so she could pass – if she wanted to leave.

She wouldn't go. I knew she wouldn't.

She brushed past me. I trailed after her down the hall and into the kitchen, where, with no wasted motion, she put on her coat and her cloche hat. Was she waiting for me to say something?

"...You always leave it to me," she said – not hurtfully, just stating a simple truth. "I love you, Ned, but you've got to start carrying some of the weight."

"I will. I promise." It was all I could say.

Daisy shifted the suitcase from hand to hand. "Why should I stay? Give me one good reason. And don't tell me you love me. I know you do. That's not the question."

Second after second ticked by.

"Say something. I'm waiting."

I couldn't open my mouth.

And she left.

Daisy –

You asked me for a reason why you should stay. My answer is in these pages. I don't expect it'll work. You ignore my letters and telegrams, refuse to talk on the telephone. I'll leave this notebook with Mathilde and you can read it – or not read it – as you like.

I can't say it any more directly than this:

Forgive me.

Come home.

It's a lonely world, my darling.

Let's not go through it alone.

Your Ned

— 13 —

April 27, 1979
93 River Road
Point Pleasant, PA

The late afternoon sun slants obliquely through the window. Soon I'll start a small fire in the living room. It's almost May, but it gets chilly as the day moves toward evening and the trees darken. Dusk brings mist from the Delaware and, later, deer will roam through the backyard. Stars will shine through the branches and the moon will flood our bedroom with light as bright as day.

I've closed the ancient notebook with its yellowing pages and youthful scrawl. The new notebook, purchased last week at the general store down the street, is open before me. I set down my pen and lean back in my chair.

I try not to dwell on that last agonizing night in the Doylestown hospital. She was all bones by then. I held her in my arms until I felt her heart stop, and I was left with nothing.

I rise from my desk and step outside to survey the back garden sloping down to the Delaware canal.

One beautiful morning several months after Daisy's death, Annabelle and I scattered her ashes among the lavender bushes. It's what she wanted. "That way I'll always be there with you," she'd said.

Yes, my darling, you will. Always and all ways.

I go back inside the empty house.

Sandy Shelton-Drake was convicted for the murder of Harry Burke. He'd done it, Sandy told the judge, because Burke had been blackmailing

169

him over a secret love affair. Three months into his sentence, Sandy died of a massive heart attack. He was 49 years old.

Allan Herbert left the diplomatic corps in 1923. He and Roy Carpenter went to live in Spain and, like Daisy and me, they returned to America as the war in Europe began. Allan taught high school in a suburb of Boston. Roy worked for the telephone company. We saw them on occasion when they'd train into Manhattan to see a play on Broadway, but those occasions grew less frequent and ended when Daisy and I moved to Bucks County. I haven't heard from him in – eleven years. I kept the letter he sent after Daisy's death. "I've been searching for something," he wrote,

> to blunt the agony of your loss. But I can think of nothing
> that will be of help. Time is the only consolation;
> eventually it allows us to think of the missing loved one
> without the ever-present ache of the newly bereaved. It
> transforms absence, but it can't bring her back. I don't
> believe in heaven or in hell or in any kind of afterlife.
> I'm glad this is all there is – because it's enough; and
> if it isn't, we've failed ourselves. I'll close here with an
> observation of George Bernard Shaw's. (I forget where I
> read or heard it – my mind isn't what it used to be, but
> then what is these days?) Certain people, Shaw said, are
> so important to us that their lives end not with their deaths,
> but with ours. Perhaps some part of Daisy's spirit lives on
> in us. That's the only kind of immortality I can believe in.

Lawson Peters and I met every once in a while for a bottle of red-eye at the Closerie des Lilas or the Deux Magots, but all we talked about was our time in the service and the murder of Harry Burke. Lawson died of a stroke in 1962, a bigwig in the FBI. His obituary was on the front page of *The New York Times*.

A decade after Burke's murder, I went into a bar near the Canal St. Martin to kill a half-hour before meeting a publisher. A shadow fell across my *Paris-Soir*. I looked up to see a disheveled and weaving figure: Inspector Hilaire. It took me a moment to realize this was the compact, dandyish man who'd once tried to slam me behind bars. He was too boiled to speak, but there was hatred in his eyes. He wobbled away and out the door. It was only later I realized the date was November 11 – Armistice Day. His son was dead. And I was alive.

170

Beatrice remained our dear friend in France and later in America. She lives in Flemington, NJ, sixteen miles from here. I see her often. She's as striking and vibrant as she was sixty years ago, though her once-black hair is now white. I am a relatively distinguished figure, or so I believe, even though *my* once-black hair is mostly gone. We make a handsome couple when we meet for dinner in Lambertville or sit on a park bench beside the Delaware and reminisce. I'm sure we're often mistaken for an old married couple. There is some small truth to that observation; we are joined by a shared past. And by our love for Daisy.

Marcel became a celebrity in France on December 10, 1919, when he was awarded the Prix Goncourt for *Within a Budding Grove*, the second volume of his extraordinary novel. His fame was immediate and widespread – such was the power of the word in those days. It made little difference to Marcel; he labored through the nights to complete his opus and took his sudden fame in stride. He'd long realized what was truly important to him: his book. Nothing would interfere with that, not even the plaudits of the literary world he'd yearned for as a young socialite.

The only thing that interfered was death. Marcel died in 1922. A cold turned into influenza and, untreated, influenza turned into pneumonia. Marcel refused medical treatment up to the very end. Various biographers have speculated on his unwillingness to take care of himself. Some view it at as a mystical union of author and book, as his death came shortly after he wrote the words "the end." With the manuscript finished, he had no reason to continue living. Others viewed his demise as a form of suicide; he was a self-hating half-Jewish homosexual who couldn't bear the weight of his compromised existence, so he drove himself into the grave.

I believe he died by accident. He had his way in every other matter, pampered by a doting mother, insulated from the world by an inheritance of millions. What Marcel wanted, he got. Why should his health be any different? In the end, he miscalculated. He'd overestimated his strength. Marcel couldn't admit that something might not be subject to his wishes – even mortality.

I think about these people.

And miss them all, the living and the dead.

I went to the basement workroom to put the notebook away. Re-arranging the tissue paper that lined the trunk, I found something I'd never seen before. Under the paper was a sealed envelope, my name on the front in Daisy's handwriting.

Finding her gloves had been an unexpected gift. This envelope was another. The gloves had transported me into a world I'd thought was lost forever. Where would this letter take me?

I opened the envelope and read its contents in the evening chill of my empty workroom.

June 3, 1968

Dear Ned,

The doctors told me what I've already guessed: I have very little time.

I am afraid.

Not so much for myself, but for you, my darling. I wonder how you'll get along without me. Do I flatter myself? Perhaps. But I know you. You're a kind and loving man and a fine writer, but you've never moved through this world with ease. You needed me to help, and I did, with all the love I had. I don't quite know how to say what I want to say. So I'll state it flatly.

I killed Harry Burke.

His demands were tearing Allan to pieces. I couldn't bear to see my brother suffering so. I knew Burke's demands would never let up. I also knew where Sandy kept his revolver and, when the party reached its height, I shot that vile creature.

I thought I'd gotten away with it until you told the police about Burke's dying words. I was shocked that he lived long enough to accuse me. Then you betrayed me and wrecked my plan to save Allan. And all because of jealousy. You didn't trust me. You didn't trust our love. And so you betrayed me.

When Beatrice visited me in jail, I confessed. I couldn't carry that burden alone. Beatrice asked if she could tell Sandy, and I agreed.

She came back the next day with the idea that saved me.

"We talked it over," Beatrice said. "Sandy wants to take your place."

Beatrice explained that Sandy had suffered from rheumatic fever as a child and his heart was severely damaged. A few weeks before the party, he'd been to his doctor. The news was bad: Sandy's heart was failing. He had little time left. He'd take the blame for Burke's murder and spend what time he had left behind bars. Sandy hadn't had an affair so Burke had no cause to blackmail him.

At first I refused. But Beatrice insisted. I must let Sandy go through with it. The only answer he'd accept was "yes."

Eventually I agreed.

We explained the situation to Marcel, who saw no reason I should sacrifice my life for taking Burke's. And so he gathered us together and "proved" Sandy was the murderer. We played our parts brilliantly, I think, especially Sandy, with his bluster and fake suicide attempt. Allan, Albrecht Schneider, Lawson Peters and Hilaire had no clue what we were doing.

It came off without a hitch.

I didn't think Marcel's "solution" would convince anyone, frankly; it struck me as ludicrous, a wildly-careening boat destined to destroy itself on the rocks of Credibility.

I was wrong.

It only proves the old maxim: no one wants to see a beautiful woman go to jail.

And I was beautiful in those days. Wasn't I? I was released, and Sandy went to prison.

All these years later, when I think of what they did to help me — to help us — I am overwhelmed by their love and their bravery. Sandy surrendered his life because he loved Beatrice. Beatrice let him do it because she loved me.

I wanted to be free because I love you.

You didn't make it easy. Your suspicions twisted your thinking and hurt me terribly. No one means more to me than you. I thought I proved that every day. Turning me over to the police tore a wound in me I was sure would never heal.

It took time, but the wound healed. I saw how much Beatrice and Sandy loved each other — saw Sandy's sacrifice — and realized that I loved you just as deeply. My love was powerful enough to encompass your fear and anger. After a great deal of coaxing on Beatrice's part, I read your explanation. I saw how much you love me and what drove you to do what you did. To understand is to forgive, as the ancients say. I understood…and forgave you. I came home.

I've never been afraid of my actions or their consequences. I'd have proudly owned up to killing Burke except for one reason:

You. You were still reeling from the War. Holding you in my arms, I could feel the torment of your nightmares. I thought you were dying. I wasn't sure you'd be alive when I woke up. I knew you thought of killing yourself and, truth to tell, sometimes I wished you had. Then I'd berate myself for having such awful thoughts. I considered borrowing money from father so you could go to a sanatorium. Something drastic had to be done. During those awful days I'd ask myself: What keeps him alive?

It may sound like bragging, but I knew it was me. I had to save you. To do that, I had to stay out of prison. Don't think harshly of us. Don't think harshly of me. I love you — I love you most of all.

You may never read this. Part me of hopes you never will. I place it here, in this box of mementos. I forgave you, my darling Ned. I ask you now to forgive me.

I am

Your Daisy, always and all ways

173

Once, many years ago, Marcel asked: "Has Daisy ever disappointed you?"

My answer was no, she hadn't.

Surprised me? Oh, yes.

When she returned at last and lifted me out of the morass of sorrow I'd been drowning in.

And tonight. She surprised me tonight. I see it now – how she did it, how *they* did it, how they fooled us all.

Daisy lived with what she'd done for almost forty years. She killed one man to save another – to save several men: Allan, me, and the other victims of Burke's vile practices who might have been driven to suicide by a blackmailer's horrendous demands.

"If there was ever any question of a debt, it's been paid in full…"

I sit here in the living room of the house I'll leave in the morning. Logs crackle and hiss in the fireplace. I hold her letter in my hands. What to make of it? Such devotion, such love. Page by page, I feed her letter to the fire.

174

— 14 —

In his book Marcel argued for the primacy of memory over experience. According to him, a person or an event is only truly experienced in recollection; what we thought had been lost forever can, in an instant, be recaptured fully in memory.

I don't want a memory recaptured by involuntary means. I don't want a memory at all. I want Daisy. I want my love.

I can't have that, so I must settle for what I have:

An old steamer trunk with its peeling decals and faded Cunard luggage tags. The feel of my old notebook pages, the life those pages contain. Tucked in between the pages, an ancient sheet of onionskin paper, typed on a Remington Streamliner manual portable. A few fading photographs.

A pair of opera gloves.

I watch Daisy as she pulls one glove on, then the other, rolling and smoothing the satin along her forearms, then holding her hands out to study them in the tremulous gaslight of our bedroom on the Rue Daguerre when we were young and in love and death was far away...

Photograph of Joseph Goodrich: Vera Hoar

About the Author

JOSEPH GOODRICH is a playwright whose work has been produced across the United States, in Canada and Australia, and published by Samuel French, Playscripts, Padua Hills Press, and Applause Books, among others. His adaptations of *The Red Box* and *Might As Well Be Dead* are the first officially-sanctioned stage versions of Rex Stout's Nero Wolfe stories and had their world premieres at Park Square Theater in Saint Paul, Minnesota. Canada's Vertigo Theatre produced the world premiere of his adaptation of Ellery Queen's novel *Calamity Town*, which received the 2016 Calgary Theater Critics Award for Best New Script. *Panic* received the 2008 Edgar Allan Poe Award for Best Play.

He is the editor of *People in a Magazine: The Selected Letters of S. N. Behrman and His Editors at "The New Yorker"* and *Blood Relations: The Selected Letters of Ellery Queen, 1947-1950*, which was nominated for Anthony and Agatha Awards. His fiction has appeared in *Ellery Queen's Mystery Magazine, Alfred Hitchcock's Mystery Magazine*, and two Mystery Writers of America anthologies. His non-fiction has appeared in *EQMM, AHMM, Mystery Scene*, and *Crimespree*. An alumnus of New Dramatists, an active member of MWA, and a former Calderwood Fellow at the MacDowell Colony, he lives in New York City.

Related Titles from Perfect Crime

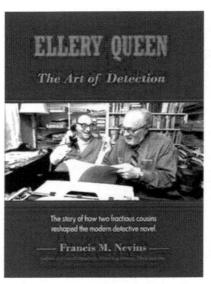

"Tempting to call this definitive."
Publishers Weekly

Memories of author/editor Fred
Dannay. With many photos.

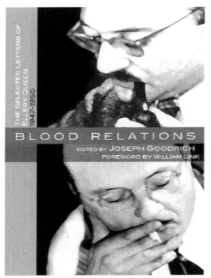

Anthony and Agatha nominee

Edgar finalist in criticism

Edgar-winner Joseph Goodrich Casts an Eye
on Some of Mystery's Finest.

Entertaining and informative." Ted Hertel, *Deadly Pleasures*
"I started to make a list of all the books mentioned in this collection that I
wanted to add to my TBR pile, but then gave up when I discovered I wanted
to read just about every book."

Profiles and appreciations of Dashiell Hammett, Rex Stout, Ellery Queen,
Nicholas Meyer, Lucille Fletcher and many more.

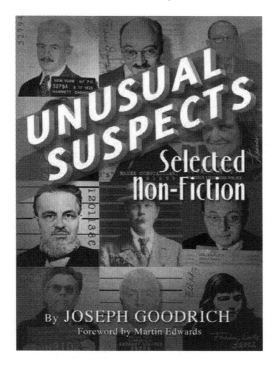

"Accurate, informative, and a pleasure to read."
Jon L. Breen   *Mystery Scene*

"Filled with gems!" *S J Rozan*

"Warmly loving and personal homage." *Rupert Holmes*

190 pages Photos $12 Trade Paperback and ebook

Made in the USA
Middletown, DE
22 September 2022

10686034R00104